This story is dedicated to my mum,

the most magical person I know.

USBORNE

KNITBONE PEPPER
GHOST DOG

A Rabbit called Wish

By Claire Barker Illustrated by Ross Collins

Contents

COLD SNAP

Knitbone Pepper glanced over at his friends; a jolly jumble of animal ghosts, huddled around the library fireplace. They snuggled together in the flickering orange glow, trying to keep warm. It was winter in Bartonshire and, as was usual for this time of year, Starcross Hall was as chilly as a penguin's pants.

Wrapped up in a tartan shawl, his beak chattering, Gabriel the goose flicked through a holiday brochure advertising "Sunshine Tours".

Valentine the hare shivered on a wobbly hot-water bottle, wearing three jumpers that he had borrowed from various old teddy bears. Martin the hamster sat in a fluffy slipper, eating hot and spicy ginger biscuits. Meanwhile Orlando, the little Elizabethan monkey, had tucked himself and a collection of his very best spoons into a woolly bedsock and was hopping up and down. In the middle of the gathering, as unique as a snowflake, sat Winifred Clementine Violet Araminta Pepper, heir to Starcross Hall.

If a passer-by had looked through the frosted windowpanes on that Friday afternoon, all they would have seen was a young girl curled up by the fireside alone. But Winnie Pepper was never alone. In fact, within the grounds of her home, she was always surrounded by this cheerful gang of ghosts. The friendly spirits of her ancestors' pets, the Beloveds had been pattering around the corridors of Starcross Hall for centuries, keeping an eye on the Peppers and getting stuck into adventures. These days Winnie was an honorary member of S.O.S. (the Spirits of Starcross) too, even though she was both human and alive, which made her feel very special. Best of all, this invisible band of chums included her very own ghost dog and best friend forever, Knitbone Pepper.

From over near the window, Knitbone gazed intently at Winnie. Watching her now in the firelight, back from school at last, her head cocooned in cosy scarves and blowing on her fingertips to keep them warm, he thought how much he loved her. He loved her more than all the frisbees, bicycle wheels and cowpats in the world, more than sticks and balls, even more than squirrels and bones. They went together like tea and toast, strawberries and cream, chips and beans. She was the icing on his bun, the cherry in his pie and he never, ever tired of worshipping her.

"Knitbone, do you want something?" Winnie asked, glancing up, feeling his starry-eyed gaze on her.

"He's always doing that," chuckled Valentine.

"Like a lovesick puppy," giggled Gabriel, not bothering to look up from his book.

"He EEZ a lovesick puppy. Loony-moony woof-face," crooned Orlando, sock-hopping over to Knitbone.

He wrapped his little monkey arms around Knitbone's leg and gave it a tight squeeze.

Martin the hamster stood up in his slipper and saluted. "Knitbone is just doing his Beloved duty. And very good he is at it too. Carry on, that dog."

"Thank you, Martin," woofed Knitbone, wagging his tail. "I certainly shall." He trotted across the bare floorboards and snuggled his head under Winnie's arm.

"I wouldn't have it any other way, Knitbone," said Winnie,

her teeth clattering in the cold air. She pulled
her scarf closer and shivered. "*Brrr*. It's very
draughty in here today, isn't it?"

Winnie put another log on the fire and
watched the golden sparks fly up the chimney.

"You'd think after selling all those Von Fluff paintings we found in the attic, that Lord and Lady Pepper might have got around to fixing the heating by now," sighed Valentine, chipping away at a frozen cup of tea.

It was true that Winnie's parents had spent some of the fortune on making rickety-rackety old Starcross Hall slightly more comfortable. But being eccentric aristocrats, they thought that *comfortable* meant more beehives and a helter-skelter, not actually fixing important things that were broken, like the leaky roof or the wonky heating. Other than a lick of paint, the house was very much as it had always been

– a higgledy-piggledy, 950-year-old tumbledown wreck.

This wasn't a problem for most of the year. In the spring, daffodils and crocuses sprang up along the brick pathways. Summertime was a season for flinging open the windows, a time for letting in sunshine, the air and the birds. Then the long golden days warmed the walls and bright green lizards basked on the front steps. The blowy autumn was just as beautiful, a coppery delight with windfall apples to munch. But it took real determination to get through a Starcross winter.

Some days it was so cold that the Peppers stayed tucked up in bed, as draughts sliced under doorways and stabbed through the chinks in the window frames. Water froze in the washing-up bowl and taking a shower felt more like braving a blizzard. There was a big old boiler in the cellar, but it was very temperamental. On the rare occasions it did work, its grumpy pipes creaked and whined in protest, sending out nothing but a whimper of warmth.

Luckily the Peppers were made of strong stuff and, from medieval times to the present day, generations had battled the cold with typical cheer. Starcross Hall was their home and all of the Peppers – both dead *and* alive – loved it whatever the weather. Winnie's parents believed the solution was to "wrap up warm, do lots of star jumps and think cosy thoughts". Indeed, Lord P simply saw it as an opportunity to wear several hats at a time and

Lady P said it was the perfect temperature to make her infamous donkey milk ice pops.

But that morning, Lord Pepper had awoken to discover his wizard hat frozen solid to his head, as firmly as an upside-down icicle, and he finally decided that enough was enough. He grabbed a fistful of cash from the biscuit tin and disappeared down the lane to catch the bus into Bartonshire, with the plan of finding a central-heating engineer. But that had been hours ago and now a veil of darkness was falling over the house.

"What can be taking Lord Pepper so long?" asked Gabriel, waddling across the room and craning his long neck to look out of the window. He cupped his wings against the glass and peered out into the gloom. "He's been gone all day."

Winnie looked at the clock on the mantelpiece. "I hope the number eight bus hasn't broken down again."

Suddenly Knitbone's nose twitched and his tail stood straight out. A deep woof rumbled up in his chest and popped out like a particularly surprising burp. "Wait a minute."

"What is it, boy?" asked Winnie, joining Gabriel and the others at the window. "Is it him?" A tiny dot appeared in the distance.

Martin took his telescope out of his utility belt and peered down the driveway. "Yes, it's Lord P, all right."

"Hooray for Dad!" cheered Winnie. "We aren't going to have to spend winter in bed after all! We'll be warm and cosy in no time!" She stood on her tiptoes and squinted through the frosty glass.

"Has he got the engineer with him?" asked Valentine, hopping up and down on the spot.

"No," said Martin adjusting the spyglass, "he's alone. But it looks like he's carrying something… It looks like…a… A *pancake*?"

Chapter 2

WISH UPON A STAR

Lord Pepper pushed open the door and took off two of his five coats. "Golly, *brrr!* Very chilly out there! Time for some beetroot tea to warm the cockles, I'd say."

"Dad!" grinned Winnie, shuffling to the hallway in her bunny slippers. "How did it go? Is that a boiler part? Is the engineer coming?" She poked her head out of the open door to hear a howling gale whipping down the drive and see a blanket of sparkling frost on the ground.

Lord Pepper said nothing. He looked at the floor. He looked at the ceiling. He looked at his fingers and he looked at his toes. He inspected a dusty corner cobweb very, very closely. In fact, he looked anywhere other than into the hopeful eyes of his daughter.

"Dad?" Winnie had a bad feeling about this. "*DAD*?" she said again.

"Well, Winnie," he said, zipping and unzipping anorak number three in a nervous manner, "you won't *believe* what happened, although I'm absolutely certain you will find it both interesting and amusing."

Winnie's heart sank. Her father, whilst very lovable and kind, had a tendency to get distracted. He wasn't the most reliable person when it came to getting things done, unless, of course, the thing that needed to be done involved hats. Then he had the focus of a cat with a fish finger.

Lady Pepper popped her head into the hallway. She was dressed in a knitted bodysuit, encased in wool from head to toe. "Ah good, you're back, Hector! Just in time to taste a fresh batch of donkey milk ice pops." She looked at the black disc on the table. "Ooo! How exciting! What treasures have you brought back from town?"

Still avoiding Winnie's gaze, Lord Pepper lifted up the disc. It was flat, a little threadbare and frayed. On the top was one word, embroidered in bright silver thread:

SALT.

"I was walking past Finbar's Antiques Emporium when this little beauty in the window caught my eye," said Lord Pepper. "It was the word SALT you see, because we are PEPPERS and I thought that was jolly amusing, hahaha."

Nobody laughed but he carried on. "You know, it was the most peculiar thing – it was almost as if it *beckoned* to me through the glass. *What harm can there be in taking a quick look, Hector?* I said to myself. I went inside and do you know what? It was exactly the amount of money I'd taken with me for the boiler engineer! Fancy that, eh? It's fate, I tell you! I probably wouldn't have bought it right away – because you *know* how sensible I am – but then Finbar began to talk about a couple who were after it. They'd just telephoned to say they had seen it on the interwebnet and planned to drive through the night to nab it for themselves! He said if I wanted it, this would be my last chance."

He shrugged and bit his lip. "So I gave him all my money and brought it home and now it's mine and that's that."

Winnie's shoulders heaved up and down as she considered the possibility of hibernation. Bears did it after all, so how hard could it be? She cast a baleful glance at the flat object. "So, what *is* it exactly, as if I need to ask?"

Gabriel turned to Valentine and said, "I bet I know what it is."

Valentine nodded. "The chances are very high."

"Higher than a ellyflump's earhole," said Orlando.

"WHY, IT'S A HAT OF COURSE!" hooted a joyful Lord Pepper, holding it up for everyone to see.

Winnie folded her arms and raised a doubtful eyebrow. "It doesn't look much like a hat to me. It looks like a dinner plate."

Lord Pepper grinned from ear to ear. "I know, but just you wait and see!" He gave it a sharp shake and with a small *boing* it popped up.

"It's a top hat!" cried Gabriel.

"Such pretty shiny stars!" cooed Orlando.

"Isn't it perfect, Winnie?" cried Lord Pepper. "I've only got nineteen top hats in my collection right now, so this is exactly what I need for the exhibition when it reopens in the summer. Don't forget, *The Times* called 'Hats Off to Starcross' the best worst tourist attraction in the country. We must keep our visitors happy, you know."

Winnie wrapped her scarves tighter around her body and turned to leave. "I'm glad you have found something that makes you happy, Daddy, but I must say my only wish is that the heating worked."

Winnie turned back to the chilly library, followed by her loyal band of Beloveds.

"Winnie, wait," her father called.

Winnie kept shuffling, head down. "Don't worry about it, Dad, I'll just put more vests on."

"No, Winnie – *look*!"

On the threshold of the library, she turned to look at her father.

"What is it?" she sighed. Lord Pepper had his hand on the radiator and a glowing smile on his face.

"It's the heating – feel – it's working!"

Chapter 3

WATCHDOG

Later that night, Lord Pepper carefully catalogued the hat in the Top Hat section of the museum. He locked it in a glass cabinet and went to bed, worn out with the thrilling adventures of the day.

Winnie was delighted, because for the first time in weeks she had gone to bed in only one set of clothes. Tonight everything was cosy in Starcross Hall and the grumpy old boiler seemed to have found a completely new lease of life.

Now it sang contentedly, humming along, sending warmth around the old place like a smile. It was a winter miracle.

"Turns out Dad didn't need to hire a fixer after all, eh, Knitbone?" said Winnie. "Who'd have thought the heating would start working again, just like that? And so much better than ever before." She let out a yawn, brushing the ghosts' ginger nut biscuit crumbs from the patchwork quilt. Then she wriggled beneath it, as snug as could be, whilst all the ghosts piled onto the end of Winnie's bed in their usual heap, ready to snooze the night away.

Everyone else dropped off to sleep, but Knitbone's eyelids wouldn't stay shut. Something about the house felt not quite right. He slipped out of the snoring heap and onto the floor, doing his best not to wake anyone up.

Knitbone trotted around the deserted

corridors, aware of a fizzy, niggling feeling. Like most dogs, Knitbone had a sixth sense; a sensation that told him something was about to happen and, since he'd become a ghost, that sense had only become stronger. He'd been the first to know that a ghost tiger was hiding in the Tombellini circus tent. He'd known when Moon, the sad and beautiful spirit horse, was waiting for them in the orchard. He'd known that both Krispin O'Mystery *and* William who'd turned up in the Silver Phantom had been up to no good. And now there it was again – that feeling, as if he had dust up his nose and electricity in his paw pads. But where was it coming from? He snuffled down the hallways, cautiously checking the

house, room by room, the feeling getting stronger and stronger. By the time he reached the Starcross library, Knitbone's feet were tingling furiously. He pushed open the door with his nose and peered around the door frame.

A lamp had been left on and the last embers of the fire were dying out, filling the room with a soft, honeyed light. A clock ticked-tocked on the mantelpiece and portraits of Winnie's ancestors snoozed quietly between the bookshelves. All looked perfectly normal. Then Knitbone spotted the problem: a stray top hat. It was the one that Lord Pepper had bought earlier that day, except now it was standing propped up on a side table in the library.

How did that get there? thought Knitbone. He knew for a fact it was supposed to be locked in the cabinet in the exhibition room. It had no business in here, casting its long shadow across the library. Dropping low, he crept closer to it, sniffing as he went and hoping to learn more.

The hat gave off a whiff of interesting scents; notebooks, playing cards, sixpences, Victorians, time, sorrow, seawater. And…yes…typewriter ink.

Then, just as Knitbone was within licking distance, the hat collapsed and *POP!* disappeared.

"Hey!" woofed Knitbone, swinging around.

"Where'd you go?" He looked up, he looked down, he looked all around, but the hat had completely vanished. Was this a good hat or a bad hat? Could hats even *be* good or bad? Knitbone wasn't sure. All he knew was that it was on the loose, so that counted as an Emergency Security Situation.

He galloped back upstairs and skidded into Winnie's bedroom where everyone was still fast asleep. "WAKE UP! EMERGENCY! WAKE UP! There's an escaped hat!"

"A cat?" mumbled Gabriel.

"A bat?" yawned Valentine. "Where?"

"Hand me my sword!" Martin's little beady eyes snapped wide open, always ready for a fight…

Winnie sat up, leaning on her elbows and yawning. "Hang on a second – did you say an escaped hat?"

"Yes." Knitbone did his most serious look. "Beware, Winnie. There is a dangerous and savage hat on the loose. It has broken free and it's running wild downstairs."

Orlando roly-polyed down to the bottom of the pile and wagged his finger at Knitbone. "But woof-face, strange eez normal for Starcross Hall."

"All right, I'll admit that's true," said Knitbone, "but this hat makes my fur prickle in a funny way. It's up to something. I can tell."

"Which hat is it, anyway?" said Valentine, stretching his legs. "There are thousands to choose from. We're home to the biggest hat exhibition in the world, you know. Is it a bonnet? The chef's hat? I'll bet it's the pirate's hat. Pirates are always causing trouble."

"No, no, no," whispered Knitbone. "It's the new top hat that Lord P brought home. Come on. Just get up and help me find it, please."

Winnie and the Beloveds searched the house from top to bottom. Firstly they searched the exhibition room. There was the cabinet, still locked, but it was indeed minus a hat.

"How strange," muttered Winnie. "I'm absolutely certain Dad locked it in there."

They searched the library again, under the stairs, in the airing cupboard, in the bathroom and in the downstairs coat cupboard.

They even woke up Mrs Jones in her vase in the hallway to see if she had seen it. An

extremely bad-tempered ghost
spider, Mrs Jones did not
take kindly to the
interruption and spat
curses at them until
they left her alone.

They all searched
the cellar, amongst
the saucepans in the
kitchen and even
checked the doorstep.
But the hat was
nowhere to be seen.

"Are you sure it wasn't one of your dreams?"
asked Martin, as they turned to go back to bed.
"You know, like those ones where you dream
you're chasing a squirrel and your legs go all
twitchy?"

"Dogs," sighed Valentine, rolling his eyes.
"Always overreacting."

"But I DID see it," insisted Knitbone, as they all trudged back upstairs. "And I am telling you, it was definitely *up to something*."

"Well, it's a mystery all right." Winnie yawned. "Hopefully it will turn up again by morning. Who knows?" She chuckled. "Maybe Dad decided to sleep in it."

The gang swung around Winnie's door frame, ready to tumble back into bed, when they saw something that stopped them dead in their tracks. Sitting in the middle of Winnie's bed, as if it was waiting for an appointment, was the black silk top hat.

Chapter 4

A DATE WiTH FATE

"**O**h dear," whispered Winnie, eyeing the hat with caution. "*That* wasn't there when we left."

"What should we do now?" hissed Knitbone. "Should we say something? Can hats even talk?"

"Well," replied Gabriel, "it's a *formal* hat so maybe a *formal* introduction is required." He stepped forward and gave a deep bow with his white wing.

"Ahem. Greetings, Hat. Welcome. We are

the Beloveds of Starcross Hall. Welcome to our humble home." Nothing happened, so Gabriel cleared his long throat and said it again. Still nothing.

"What if it's a baddie's hat?" asked Martin.

"What if eez a bitey hat?" fretted Orlando, hiding behind his tail. "Monkey's afeared!"

The hat began to quiver, then rock from side to side. It popped up, it popped down, it coughed and it spluttered, as if trying to start an old engine. A shower of ginger biscuit crumbs flew out of the top, settling onto Winnie's patchwork quilt. Finally, it came to a standstill. Very slowly a wispy white ear rose above the brim, followed by a thistledown pom-pom of fluff. Then two ice-blue eyes appeared, a sugar-pink nose and a pair of twitchy white whiskers. The ghostly creature cleared its throat and began.

"You are a little late, I suppose, but I am willing to overlook it on this particular occasion," he said, fixing a monocle to his eye and looking sternly at his audience.

"Greetings to you, Beloveds of Starcross Hall." His voice was firm and clipped. "If you will allow me the honour, I shall introduce myself." He gave a stiff little bow. "My name is Wish Salt. I am on a mission of the utmost importance. Do not be afraid, I mean you no harm."

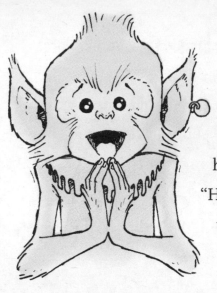

"EEZ A WICKLE GHOSTIE WABBIT!" Orlando squealed in delight and clasped his hands together. "He has a soft-and-fluffy uppy ear and a soft-and-fluffy downy ear! *He's so cute it-a make-a my tummy feel all funny inside!*"

The rabbit frowned and cleared his throat. He screwed his monocle even more firmly into his eye socket and straightened his bow tie.

"Welcome to Starcross Hall, Mr Salt," woofed Knitbone, trying to look serious and wondering how this stranger came to know who they were.

"Knitbone Pepper, I presume," said the rabbit with another small bow. "You may refer to me simply as Wish. After all, we shall be working together." Wish held out a ghostly paw to Winnie

and she leaned forward to shake it. It was soft
and small and very, very lovely – but under the
circumstances she decided it was probably best
not to say so.

"Now, down to business," said Wish briskly.
He rummaged around in the top hat, pulled out a
notebook and took a pencil from behind his ear.
He flicked through the pages. "Let me see…ah!
Here we are. I knew the reviews were in here
somewhere." He cleared his throat and read them
out loud.

"'Winnie, Knitbone and the gang made our dream come true. Highly recommended.' Roojoo the ghost tiger and Bertie, ringmaster, Tombellini Circus. *'Without the Spirits of Starcross we would never have found each other.'* Moon the ghost horse and Rosabel Starr, astronomer."

Wish peered over his monocle. "Both five-star reviews, I see. Very impressive. Am I correct in understanding that your motto is 'a Beloved in need is a friend indeed'? And is it also correct that you are experienced in dealing with difficult and perilous situations?"

The others looked at each other in confusion.

"Ah, I see. You are wondering how I know so much about you. Winnie, Gabriel, Valentine,

Martin and Orlando, not to mention the famous Knitbone Pepper, of course," said the rabbit. He put the notebook and pencil away and twitched his pink nose. "The answer is quite simple. I am like you, only different. You are merely standard Beloveds, whilst I am an Heirloom Beloved. Further information is to be found in *The Good Ghost Guide*, an excellent book I found on your library shelves earlier. Please refer to page 348. I shall wait whilst you prepare for our meeting. Chop-chop." He disappeared into the hat. Tinny waiting music began to play. The rabbit was on hold.

Gabriel gulped. "Oh. Right. We'd better get it then. Winnie, lend me a hand?" Gabriel waddled out of the bedroom, followed by Winnie. Very soon they were back with a big heavy book. Gabriel laid it down on the floor and turned to the correct page. Everyone crowded around the book as Gabriel read out loud.

Heirloom Beloveds

Description: Career Beloved.
An expert professional, devoted to
a family rather than one special person.
Unusual gifts. Driven by duty not love.
Organized and Loyal.
Natural warriors.

The waiting music stopped abruptly and the rabbit popped up again, brushing ginger biscuit crumbs from his whiskers. "Ready? Yes? Now? Good. Now you know *who* I am, and *what* I am. You will be glad to hear that at last the stars have aligned, the fates are in tune and the time is RIGHT."

"What on earth is he going on about?" said Valentine to Gabriel. "A natural warrior? He's just a bunny."

There were times when Valentine, a wild hare, had been mistaken for a rabbit and, frankly, it got on his nerves. Hares were noble, golden-eyed, long-legged speed wonders with tall, beautiful ears. A rabbit was a chunky, dumpy, droopy hop-along that chomped carrots. How anyone could put them in the same bracket bewildered him.

"Listen, rabbit." Valentine looked down his long brown nose at Wish. "As you are so keen to point out, you are NOT like us – you are driven by duty not love. Beloveds can't be handed down like crockery, you know. They belong to a special person. Salts and Peppers, like pepper and salt – we are quite different, I think. I haven't even heard of an Heirloom Beloved." He folded his arms and turned away. "In fact, I've never heard such nonsense in all my eight centuries. Anyway, what sort of animal lives in a *hat*?"

Wish glared hard at Valentine through his

monocle. Then he turned to Winnie, who was shifting awkwardly from slipper to slipper. "Winifred Clementine Violet Araminta Pepper, are you feeling cosy?"

Winnie looked nervously at Knitbone. "Erm, yes, I am, thank you. Why?"

Wish turned back to Valentine and said, "Who *precisely* do you think mended the boiler?"

"I beg your pardon?"

"I said, WHO do you think is responsible for making the Peppers so suddenly comfortable in draughty old Starcross?"

Valentine looked uneasy. "Well, I don't know, but it can't be you unless— Oh!" A thought crossed Valentine's mind like a big cloud moving across the sun. The book had said that Heirloom Beloveds had special gifts. "Oh dear," said Valentine. "I see."

"Yes, HARE," said Wish Salt, now apparently reading his mind. "You are correct. I granted that wish of Winnie's." He gave a deep bow. "You are not dealing with any old bunny from a burrow, you know. In future I'll thank you to remember you are dealing with a *professional magician*."

Chapter 5

TRUE NORTH

Wish Salt was indeed very professional. In fact, inside his hat he appeared to have a whole office. In it he kept timetables, files, charts and newspaper clippings. He even had an old clickety-clacking typewriter on which to compose important letters. Gabriel, a librarian, was hugely impressed by the levels of organization, not to mention the range of stationery.

Knitbone couldn't help feeling a little

concerned. How were they, a raggle-
taggle gang of biscuit-scoffing
ghosts, supposed to help?
He wondered if now
was a good time to
mention that they
once lost Orlando in
the cutlery drawer?

"Right," said the rabbit. "We need to
get down to the details of exactly how
you will help me. I understand your special
expertise lies in the area of reuniting a Beloved
with a special person here at Starcross Hall, yes?"

"Well," Winnie said, looking doubtful, "yes,
but we've only ever done it twice. Three times,
if you count me and Knitbone. But I wouldn't say
we are experts."

"Nonsense," said Wish, waving a piece of
paper in the air. "Heirloom Beloveds only work
with the best in their field."

"Oh good, because I like fields," piped up Knitbone, his tail suddenly wagging. "And parks. And squirrels too. Although I don't like park-keepers or suitcases so I hope there won't be any of those."

"Oh yes, well, my problem is this," said Wish. "I have lost a boy."

"A boy?" asked Winnie. "Oh dear."

"Yes, the last of the Salts." Suddenly there was a strong smell of peppermint and the rabbit turned away in embarrassment. The ghosts looked at each other in surprise. Was Wish blushing beneath his fur?

"When did you lose this boy?" asked Martin.

"I lost him when he was a baby." The rabbit sharply shuffled his paperwork as the distinctive minty whiff of ghost shame filled the room. "I'm afraid I've failed in my duty. Heirloom Beloveds aren't supposed to make errors."

Orlando swung himself onto the bed and

climbed onto the rim of the hat. "Don't be sad,
Mister Bunny," said Orlando. "Everybody make
mistake. Once Orlando sat on a buzzy bee."
He let out a big sigh at the memory. "Monkey
bottom *spicy-spicy*."

"You don't understand," insisted Wish. "He is the *last* of the Salts. I must find him and tell him, or the family line will be broken forever. It is our destiny. We belong together, you see. However," he said, forcing a smile, "the good news is, I believe he is nearby. But for some reason I'm having terrible trouble getting close to him. So I need your help."

"Is he near Starcross?" asked Knitbone.

"Definitely. In fact, even closer today than yesterday," said Wish. He rummaged around in the hat and took out a brass compass. "See where this points? See how it vibrates?" The others looked closely at the compass and saw that where north should be it simply said, *Ernest Salt.*

"How old is he?" asked Gabriel.

"He is ten years, forty-seven days, fifteen hours and forty-seven minutes old," said Wish. "Approximately." He looked up and down at Winnie, his eyes widening. "In fact, about your age. Maybe you have met him."

"Ernest Salt?" Winnie shook her head. "Sorry, never heard of him."

Wish squeezed his eyes shut, deep in thought. After a minute he opened them again and stared hard at the trembling compass. "Are you sure?"

"There aren't even any S's in my class," said Winnie, counting the names on her fingers. "The register goes me, then Billy Quiggle, then Lily Rabinowitz, then Jack Toffington, then Isabel Uffchurch. I'd remember a name like Ernest Salt." She looked down at the rabbit. "Maybe you've made a mistake?"

Wish frowned. "I am not in the habit of making mistakes, Winnie Pepper. The fact is, he is here and I *shall* find him because he *must* fulfil his destiny and *that* is *that*."

Knitbone cocked his head to one side. "Destiny? Why do you keep saying that?"

Wish hopped out of the hat and thumped his foot impatiently on the floorboards. "Must I keep repeating myself? He is the last of the SALTS. Ernest is destined to become the greatest stage magician in England!"

Chapter 6

A FAMILY AFFAIR

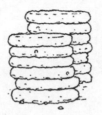

Martin gathered together a big plate of ginger nuts and everyone settled down on the bed.

"There is much to explain," sighed Wish impatiently. "To save time I shall show you one of my Magic Memory reels. Please pay close attention to what you are about to see."

There was a whir of a projector and a brilliant shaft of light shot out the side of the hat. A black and white film flickered on Winnie's bedroom

wall. A man with black curly hair, dressed in Victorian clothing, was browsing the shelves of a harbourside stall, inspecting silver jugs, rugs, candles and lanterns.

"Gosh!" said Winnie. "That looks like it was a long time ago."

"Who's he?" demanded Martin, pointing his sword at the man.

"That is the magician, Joseph Salt," announced Wish. "The year is 1864 and he is waiting for his ship to sail from Zanzibar to London."

The man picked up a flat black disc and gave it a shake. Up popped a top hat, frayed at the edges, embroidered with stars. He fished in his pocket for some coins, paid the stallholder, squashed it flat and put it in his bag.

"Isn't that your hat?" asked Martin, spraying crumbs everywhere.

"Correct. When Joseph got back home to

London and popped the hat back up again,
he discovered that it contained rather more than
he bargained for," said Wish, pointing at the image
with a stick. "Kindly observe."

The scene changed. Here was Joseph again,
but now he was staring down into the hat in
amazement and taking out a brown cardboard
label.

The film showed Joseph reaching into the
hat and lifting out a fluffy white rabbit, one ear
up, one ear down, wearing a monocle and
bow tie.

"Quickly, Joseph realized that the hat and I
were a dynamite combination," recounted Wish.
"Not only could we disappear, but together we
could also make things appear – bunches of roses,
bottles of wine, cuckoo clocks. He asked me if I
would be interested in going into the family
business. Of course I agreed – a magic-hat rabbit
must have a profession – and he stitched the

name SALT into the top of the hat, sealing our union. Together we were stronger than ever. Joseph Salt's Magic Show became a huge success around the country."

The scene changed to a theatre, full of applause and candlelight. Wish smiled and pressed his snowy little paws together at the memory. "I lived with the Salt family all my life. We were devoted to each other."

The scene changed

again to a family posing for a portrait; four children, Joseph and his wife. In the very centre, held aloft by Joseph was the hat, Wish striking a formal pose from within.

Wish let out a deep sigh. "But a rabbit, even a rare magic-hat rabbit, cannot remain alive for ever. One day, when I was very old and no longer had an appetite for even the best of carrots, I knew the time had come to say goodbye."

"Uh-oh," said Orlando, taking out a hanky and blowing his nose loudly. "Now we a-comin' to the sobby bit."

"Joseph made me a soft bed of hay in my hat," continued Wish, "and thanked me for all I had done. He made a wish; that I would never leave them. He wished that my spirit would remain in the hat, that I would watch over his children, and his children's children." Wish stood up very straight and tall. "And so – because as I think I may have mentioned, I was rather unusual in my talents – his wish was granted. It was then that I transformed into an Heirloom Beloved. As Joseph's family grew, imagine their amazement as the miracles continued to happen. Balloons, riding boots, unicycles – they all popped out of my hat on a regular basis." He smiled. "I may have died, but that wasn't going to stop me turning up for work. And although they were not able to see me any more, they passed the secret on to each other, knowing my spirit was with them.

"My hat was handed down from generation to generation," explained Wish, "and the name Salt became famous amongst magicians. The family kept it close wherever they went, keeping me safe from wicked thieves, never letting me out of their sight. But one stormy day, fate tore us apart."

The film changed to full colour. A yacht was being tossed about on moonlit waves. "It's called *The White Rabbit!*" cried Winnie.

"Ten years ago, Ernest's mother, Marigold Salt, was sailing to a magician's fair in Ireland when the boat began to sink." Wish shook his head and wrung his paws in anguish. "I tried so hard to fix it but it turns out that my magic isn't very reliable in the wet. In the end it was hopeless. Marigold kissed baby Ernest and placed his christening wand in his chubby fist. Tucking him carefully into my hat, she whispered, 'Take care of him, Wish.' Then she waved us goodbye."

The scene changed again to a baby, bobbing out to sea in a top hat.

"I'm afraid Marigold was never seen again," said Wish, his voice grave and flat. The film whirred to a sudden stop and the light went off.

Winnie wiped away a tear. "That's so sad. But what about you?"

"That morning the three of us – hat, ghost and baby – washed up on a sandy beach, relieved to be safe at last. But then – disaster! Baby Ernest saw a pretty shell in the distance and crawled out of my hat." Wish tugged at his ears in distress. "Then a wave came and washed me and my hat back out to sea!"

"OH NO! Poor Ernest!" cried Martin.

"Poor Ernest, indeed," said Wish. "He had nothing in the world save for a nappy and a small wand. I drifted helplessly away on the waves, pulled out by the tide, frantically trying to jump-start my hat. But then – oh, the relief! From far away I spotted two people running down the beach and my heart filled with hope.

'Take good care of him,' I called, 'for he is the last of the Salts! I will be back for him very soon!' Although of course they couldn't hear me. Then, at the worst possible moment, my hat suddenly went into lockdown and everything went black."

"What happened then?" asked Knitbone.

"Oh, it's a long and sorry tale, I'm afraid. I was caught up in the Atlantic Ocean in a fisherman's nets. He gave me to his wife, who used me as a teapot stand – most embarrassing. Since then, I've been all over the country, from charity shops to car-boot sales to antiques fairs, popping short distances, here and there. For years I've been trying to track down Ernest with my compass, but the boy keeps moving. One minute he is in Scotland, the next in Wales or London. It's exhausting. But I must keep going. I have to find him."

"Can't you just wish him here? Fix

everything? Like you did with the heating?" asked Winnie.

"Unfortunately, Winnie Pepper, I cannot make that sort of wish for myself – not to mention the fact that my magic simply isn't as strong without a Salt by my side. Worse, it seems like every time I get close to him, my hat collapses flat, sometimes locking me in for days. I have to keep a supply of ginger biscuits as I could be marooned at any time."

Martin looked suitably impressed and stuffed his cheeks with a couple of emergency biscuits – just in case.

"The thing is," said Wish, "the poor old thing is rather like a wonky banger these days, coughing and spluttering along, turning up in the wrong places." Wish sighed, stroking its threadbare rim. "Frankly, I've been at my wit's end about what to do." His eyes brightened. "Then – wonder of wonders – I heard about the Beloveds of Starcross Hall!"

"And how exactly did you hear of us?" asked Valentine.

"I met a ghost horse at a travelling fair," explained Wish. "She told me all about how you'd helped her to find her person and she gave me this." He dived down into the hat and came back up with a newspaper clipping all about the Starcross hat exhibition, featuring a cheesy photo of the Peppers. "At last, I had a solution to my problem! I studied the photograph carefully and, with a lot of effort, managed to steer my hat closer and closer to Bartonshire. The closest I could get was Finbar's Antiques Emporium in the high street. By complete luck, I spotted Lord

Pepper through the window! Knickerbockers and a wizard hat makes a man easy to spot! I thought I would need to engage all of my hypnotic powers to guarantee the sale, but to my amazement, Lord Pepper put a fistful of cash on the shop counter without the slightest hesitation. Really *most* surprising."

Winnie and Knitbone rolled their eyes. That was by far the least surprising thing they'd heard all night.

Chapter 7

LOST SOUL

The next morning Winnie woke up to the sound of shouting in the hallway and a slammed door. What on Earth was going on? She rolled over and picked up her alarm clock. She sat bolt upright, jolted out of her thoughts. "My goodness! Is that the time? Look, everyone – we've overslept!"

"Well, that's what happens when you spend all night hanging out with a magic bunny," said Martin, sliding down the bedcovers and landing on the floor with a bump.

"Speaking of Wish, where's he got to?" asked
Valentine, peeking out of the patchwork quilt
and looking around. "He's vanished again."

Winnie dragged on her dressing gown and
they all shuffled downstairs to quickly check on
Wish's hat. Sure enough, there it was, collapsed
flat in the locked cabinet, as if it had never left.

"Well, that answers that question," said
Winnie. "Come on, everyone, let's get
some breakfast and find out who
was making all that racket
on the doorstep."

Winnie entered the
kitchen to see her mother
energetically stirring
a big vat of porridge.
"Oh, darling,
there you are,"
said Lady Pepper,

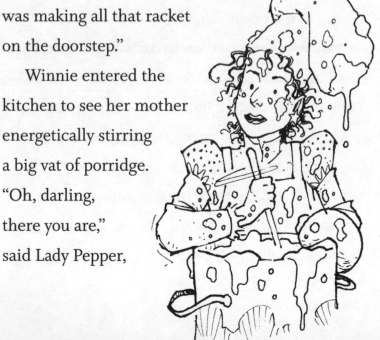

frowning into the pan. "Did the noise wake you? A pair of awful strangers were at the door *demanding* to buy your father's new hat. They insisted they had already reserved it on the phone at Finbar's Antiques Emporium so it was theirs by right. Very pushy indeed, peering into the house, jamming their foot in the door. The woman was wearing a dreadful moth-eaten fur coat and the man reeked of cigars. I told them I was far too busy working on this new dish for my vegan recipe book, *Yeasts Not Beasts*, to discuss hats, and sent them packing." She finally looked up at Winnie. "Would you like a bowl of my yummy mushroom porridge? I think it's just about perfect now." Heaving beige lava bubbled and glopped in the pan.

"Er...actually...I think I'll just have cornflakes today, thanks," said Winnie, grabbing a box, a bowl and a spoon. "Can't stop, things to do!" They all scampered back upstairs and shut

Winnie's bedroom door behind them.

Springing into guard-dog mode, Knitbone dashed over to the window and put his paws on the sill. In the distance he watched two figures disappear down the drive, shouting and shoving each other. Who were they?

"Whoever they are I don't like the look of them," he growled to himself. "Good riddance and don't come back."

"Knitbone, come over here. We've got work to do," said Gabriel, as they gathered around him on the rug. "How are we going to help Wish find this Ernest boy? Only Winnie can leave Starcross, you know the rules, so it could be tricky."

Winnie crunched a mouthful of cornflakes. "I'm not sure what help that is anyway. He's definitely not at my school and Bartonshire only has one. I suppose he *might* be home-schooled." She lowered her voice to a whisper. "*Either that or Wish has just made another mistake.*"

"Heirloom Beloveds hardly ever make mistakes." The hat appeared on the rug and Wish popped out of the top, making everyone jump.

"Could you stop doing that, please?" gasped Valentine, clutching his chest. "At least get a bicycle bell or something to warn us you are on your way."

Wish began to pull spools of paper out of the hat. "I would have been here earlier, only my silly hat locked me in again for some reason. Most annoying. Anyway, down to business. These reports confirm what I am saying – Ernest Salt is very close." He licked his paw and held it up, as if he was testing the direction of the wind.

"Yes, very close. I'd say only half an hour away at most." He turned to Winnie, adjusting his monocle. "You must find him and bring him here. Today. I absolutely insist on it."

"But…but where shall I look?" implored Winnie.

Knitbone had an idea. "We used the computer to find Rosabel Starr for Moon. Could we try that?"

"Oh yes," honked Gabriel. "We could giggle it and maybe his name will pop up. The interwebnet is very useful like that. Let's go!"

Winnie got dressed, and then they all gathered around the computer downstairs.

It took a while for it to warm up because Lord
Pepper had connected it to a rowing machine to
generate the electricity.

Winnie pulled and slid back and forth, rowing
furiously whilst the others cheered her on. They
even waved flags on the sidelines. The whole
process was exhausting to say the least.

"Right," said Winnie, red-faced and sweating from her exertions. "Ten minutes of rowing should have put in enough charge for a few searches. Quick."

She typed the words BARTONSHIRE ERNEST SALT into the search engine. They all looked closely at the screen. It came up with articles on marshes, herrings and crisps, but nothing about a missing boy. They were about to try another angle when the computer went *bink* and turned itself off.

"Well," sighed Knitbone, "so much for that. According to the World Wide Web, there are no Ernest Salts in Bartonshire."

"Well, then the World Wide Web doesn't know what it's talking about," snapped Wish. "I know my job and I'm telling you, Ernest is very close indeed. Why don't we look in the local newspapers?"

A voice sang from the hallway. "Just popping

out to the shops," cried Lady Pepper. "I've run out of stinkhorn mushrooms again. Does anybody need anything?"

Martin sprang to his feet and clasped his little paws together anxiously. "Oh yes, Winnie! We are down to our last fifty-seven packets of ginger nuts," he said. "You absolutely *must* buy some more as a matter of urgency. No other biscuit makes a ghost feel more alive! What if we are ever marooned?"

Winnie smiled and scratched Martin behind his tiny ear. He was a very brave little hamster, but the fear of running out of snacks was strong. "Wait for me, Mum," she called. "I'm coming too."

Martin looked relieved, but Knitbone's tail drooped in disappointment, like it always did whenever Winnie went out. He wished he could follow her, like in the old days, trotting close behind her bike.

Winnie turned to the Beloveds with a smile. "Be good while I'm away. And don't worry, Knitbone, I won't be long. I've just got to pop into the public library anyway. I've had an exciting phone message from Library Jane telling me my new astronomy books are in. See you later!"

Winnie and her mother cycled off into the distance, leaving everyone else to search through piles of old newspapers in the quest to find the missing boy.

Everyone, that is, except for Knitbone, who stared forlornly out of the window, waiting for the clanks of Winnie's returning pedals.

"There's someone here called Mr Eric Salting," said Gabriel, holding up a newspaper clipping. "But he's an old man."

"And there's an advert here for a business called Ernest Engineers," said Valentine.

"No," said Wish impatiently, "these won't do at all. His name is Ernest Salt, plain and simple."

Martin flicked through old parish newsletters. "Do you know what he looks like now? After all, he went missing when he was a baby."

"Oh, I'll know him when I see him all right, don't you worry." Wish tapped his head with his paw. "Like an elephant, a rabbit never forgets."

"Oooh! I like the sound of an ellyflump bunny," crooned Orlando, his eyes twinkling. He reached out his fingers, hoping to stroke Wish's soft fur.

"*Please* control your monkey!" said Wish, diving down into the hat. "May I remind you once again, I am a *professional* rabbit. I am not available for stroking *or* cuddles *or* hugs."

Orlando stuck out his bottom lip in a sulk. "Beloveds loff hugs."

Wish shuffled his papers and adjusted his monocle. "Yes, well, that's as maybe," he said in a prim tone. "But as I have told you *more than once*, I'm not an ordinary Beloved, so kindly keep your distance. We are quite different. Pepper and Salt, Salt and Pepper, remember? Yes? Hmm? So it's paws off, thank you very much." He tutted under his breath.

Orlando took a spoon out of his handbag and looked at his smiling reflection in it.

"Funny bunny will change his mind," he crooned to the spoon. "Just you wait and see. Nobody escape Orlando's special kisses for long."

Chapter 8

SPIDER VENOM

"It's only been an hour," said Martin encouragingly. "She'll be back soon." But Knitbone continued to press his nose to the window.

Knitbone couldn't help his doggy devotion – he missed Winnie so badly when she wasn't there. Her absence was an ache in his heart and a twinge in his tail. Every day he counted the hours until she would be home from school. At least he could still walk her to and from the bus stop every day, even though he could go no further. He knew the rules: that Beloveds were tied to their home, to the place they were happiest when they were alive. If they tried to cross the Starcross estate boundaries then they risked being dissolved for ever. Whilst he was grateful to have any sort of afterlife at all, Knitbone also knew this meant he wouldn't be going into Bartonshire to run about in the park ever again, or be able to visit Library Jane or pop into the cosy Lantern Cafe with Winnie.

While Knitbone was thinking these sad thoughts, a grey spider dropped down from the ceiling on a grey wispy thread, stopping level with Knitbone's ear. A ghost and an all-round Bad Egg, Mrs Jones was always very keen to ruin anyone's day.

"Oh dear, oh dear. Oh *boo* and *hoo*. Winnie not back yet?" she whined. "She's probably having *such* an exciting time in town. That new

library is very modern,
I hear. Much better
than our dusty old
one here. Probably
full of interesting
people too. Oh!
I've just had a
terrible thought,"
she said, her eight
eyes wide open in
fake horror. "You
don't suppose in all
the excitement she's
forgotten about you, do you?"

Knitbone tried to look brave. "Don't be stupid.
Winnie would never forget about me. Go away."

"Oh yes, I'm sure you're right, Knickerface
Pickle," said Mrs Jones, careful to keep her voice
to a whisper so that nobody else could hear the
poisonous spite she was pouring into his ear.

"But things do change, you know," she wheedled. "I've seen it before. One day she'll grow up and then she won't need you any more." She swung even closer, clacking her fangs together. "Have you ever thought about *that*, Knik-nack Flip-flop? That she will leave you behind? Anyway, it's about time she made friends with her *own kind*, don't you think? Hmm?"

Knitbone's ears drooped and he stared miserably up the drive, as a maggot of doubt began to worm its way into his heart. Winnie would always want him as her best friend, wouldn't she? Mrs Jones was just saying mean things to upset him. No matter how good the books were in the public library, and no matter who she met, Winnie would always love him best, wouldn't she? Of course she would. Of course. *Of course.*

"MRS JONES!" honked Gabriel, spotting the spider hanging about near Knitbone's ear.

"Why are you here? What are you saying to him?"

Mrs Jones ignored Gabriel and swung over to Wish like a wrecking ball, hell-bent on more damage. "You'll never find this Ernest brat, you know. It'll be like looking for a needle in a haystack. Even if you did he probably won't want you anyway, after you abandoned him. It's just a stupid idea from a stupid bunch of stupid ghosts who…"

But before she could say any more, Wish grabbed her in his bunny fist, popped her in a jar and screwed the lid on tight.

"Your assistance will not be required in this matter," he said, dropping the whole thing in the wastepaper basket. "Thank you and good day, Madame Jones. I shall release you when it suits me." He returned to his paperwork, as if her spite was nothing but a mild irritation. The other Beloveds were wildly impressed.

Meanwhile, Knitbone still had his nose pressed to the windowpane, his list of worries now considerably longer.

"Knitbone, really, do stop mooning about and come and lend a paw," called Valentine.

"All right, all right, I just need one more minute," whimpered Knitbone, scanning the horizon. "Just one more…" And then he saw Winnie, cycling through the mist, head into the wind, plaits flying, mittens gripping the handlebars.

"LOOK!" Knitbone woofed joyfully, relief flooding through him. "I told you she'd come back! I told you, didn't I?" He raced to his usual place at the front door, ready to greet her.

But when Winnie pushed open the door and stepped into the hallway, she was in too much of a rush for her usual cuddle. Instead she just gave him a quick pat on the head and strode into the Starcross library. Knitbone followed her, slightly hurt but trying not to show it. Winnie shut the door firmly behind them and turned to Wish.

"Does this boy of yours," she panted urgently, "have black curly hair?"

Wish looked up, his nose twitching. "Yes. All the Salts have black curls."

"And is he likely to be tall and gangly?"

Suddenly alert, Wish stood up in his hat. "His mother was just like that. Marigold looked like a pencil – long and thin."

Winnie's eyes sparkled. "And his christening wand – did it have two letters engraved on the side?"

Wish gasped and dropped his clipboard, clasping his little paws over his face. "Yes," he whispered, full of hope. "E and S."

And with this, Winnie triumphantly bowled the biscuits across the rug, straight into Martin's open arms. She grinned in delight and announced, "Then I think I've found him."

Chapter 9

SALTY SUMS

"I was in the hobbies section of Bartonshire public library," explained Winnie, "reading my brand-new books on black holes, when the door creaked open and a boy who I've never seen before came in. He'd got a moptop of black curls and his legs were so long his trousers barely reached his ankles. I was carrying my pile of books to the desk when I heard him ask Library Jane if he could quickly apply for a library card because he was new to the area and wanted to take out some books on magic. I happened to see over his shoulder while he was filling in the form. It said:

Ernie Carbuncle, dge ten

"Ernie Carbuncle? Ah. Oh dear, no," said Wish, his whiskers drooping in disappointment. "That's the wrong name, Winnie."

"I know, but wait," said Winnie, holding up her hand. "As he turned around in a rush to go, he accidentally bumped into me and knocked my pile of books onto the carpet. He went as pink as a shrimp. Honestly, you'd think he'd never seen a girl before." She pulled off her mittens and warmed her fingers in front of the roaring log fire in the hearth. "That was when I saw it."

"SAW WHAT?" they all chorused.

"The wand. It fell out of his pocket when he

bent over; it was a little black one with a white
top. Ebony and pearl, I think. I picked it up to
give it back, but as I handed it over, I noticed it
had two letters engraved on the side in silver."
She turned to Wish and raised her eyebrows:
"E. S."

Wish leaped out of
his hat with a
squeal and did
a somersault,
landing with a
thump. "I told you,
didn't I? I told you
that he was nearby!" He
took out his compass and gave it a thrilled shake.

"I thought it *must* be him," said Winnie. "So I
asked him about the letters on the wand but…"
She hesitated. "He didn't know what they stood
for. He just looked puzzled and muttered,
'Dunno. Easy Shop?' I don't think he has any idea

that Ernest Carbuncle isn't his real name. He has no idea he's the last of the Salts. It's going to come as a big shock to hear he's not who he thinks he is."

Wish shot a bewildered glance at Winnie. "Shock? What do you mean?"

Winnie looked very uncomfortable. "Well, what if he's happy with his adopted family? You said those people on the beach that day gave you hope. What am I supposed to say? That his life was saved by a hat? That a magic ghost rabbit is looking for him? I'm going to sound bonkers." She shifted awkwardly. "Other children think I'm odd enough as it is."

"Well, that is most regrettable but he simply must be told the truth," said Wish in a matter-of-fact way. "He's Ernest Salt of the magic family Salt. I have explained the situation in the clearest terms: it is his destiny. He has to be told."

Winnie thought for a moment. "He really is

very shy, Wish. We don't want to scare him off. News this big can't come from me." She looked down at her boots, suddenly shy too. "I'm just some scruffy kid in the public library."

"You may have a point, Miss Pepper," said Wish. "But he has no family left to tell him of his destiny and *The Good Ghost Guide* rules clearly state that reuniting can only happen within the grounds of Starcross Hall. Hmm…" Wish scratched his uppy ear with his back foot and thought for a moment. "All right, here's the plan. You will bring him here and, once we are reunited, I shall be the one to tell him the good news. Then we can get back to work in the family business. First things first, you must invite him here to tea."

Winnie gulped, panic washing over her. The truth was that, despite all the events they had put on at Starcross Hall, she'd never, ever in her whole life invited another child back for tea. She knew that whilst most people in the town were kind, others whispered about the Peppers, about how Starcross Hall was supposed to be teeming with ghosts, about what a strange family they were. She knew some of her classmates talked about her behind her back, made jokes about the hats and her peculiar packed lunches full of limpet bread and acorn crisps. How could she invite another child *here*? Other children ate shop-bought cakes and played on computers that weren't powered by rowing machines.

"Tea? Here? Just the two of us? I don't think that is a good idea, Wish," said Winnie, blushing like a beetroot. "I barely know the boy. No, no. That won't do at all."

Knitbone nodded and plonked his paw in her lap. "Winnie is absolutely right. Some *boy* coming here for tea with Winnie is the worst idea ever. She's got all the friends she needs already. Absolutely no need for any more, of that I am completely certain."

The other Beloveds exchanged knowing glances but said nothing. Wish let out a disapproving snort. He umm-ed and he aah-ed, he looked at charts, gazed into a glass ball and then spun a tiny roulette wheel. "Fine, well in that case, my sources tell me there is only one thing for it. Knitbone will have to do one of his special sums."

Knitbone thought hard. Then, as quick as a hiccup he wrote a sum on the black slate hearth.

MAGICIAN + StarCROSS
=Best Talent SHOW EVER!

"Of course!" cried Winnie, giving Knitbone's shaggy head a happy rub. "You are a clever boy. We'll put on a talent show and Ernest can enter along with lots of other people. How could a young magician resist a challenge like that? Then, when he's here, we can introduce Ernest to Wish and he can explain everything. Then they can live together happily ever after and we can all go back to normal. Phew."

"I haz talents," squealed Orlando, somersaulting around the room. "Everyone *love* my special monkey stinkers. They make the eyeballs drip with joy."

"Never mind him and his smells, look at me!" said Martin, chopping through the air with his wooden sword and getting very excited. "Parry! Advance! *Slice* and *slash* and *swipe* and *stab*! All the best soldiering skil—"

"And, as you know, I can run very, very fast," interrupted Valentine, running on the spot. "Look at this," he cried, haring back and forth through the walls in a blur of fur and brick.

"Oh, pssh. *Anyone* can do that," said Orlando, swinging from the light fitting through the mirror and out again. "Eez az easy az freezy peaz."

"Maybe if you're a ghost," laughed Winnie.

Gabriel was already reaching for his trusty clipboard. "We're rather good at putting on events, aren't we, even though I do say so myself? First the circus, then the Night of a Billion Stars, then the Junk Palace TV show. I think you will be impressed by our own organizational skills, Wish," he said, fluffing out his chest feathers. "A little Bartonshire talent show should be no problem at all. Right let's get to work."

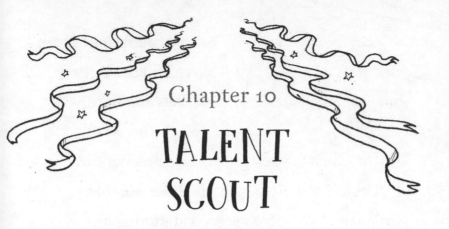

Chapter 10

TALENT SCOUT

Lord and Lady Pepper loved a party and were very enthusiastic about the idea of putting on a new event at Starcross Hall.

"We've had lots of talent shows here over the centuries," said Lord Pepper, reaching up to the shelf for a dusty old photo album. "It was the duty of the lord of the manor to put on such things for the village, you see." He turned the pages to reveal faded old photographs. There were people dressed in costumes, juggling and

doing handstands. There were others in dinner jackets singing or playing musical instruments. "It's about time we started up the tradition again, eh, Isadora? We could join in too with our own talents. Not everyone can lick their elbows and wiggle their ears, you know. Certainly not at the same time."

Lady Pepper gazed wistfully into the distance. "Once I saw a man in Paris who could play the national anthem using only his armpit. Astonishing, Hector, absolutely astonishing. I only wish you had witnessed it."

"So, I was thinking about *the prize* for the best act," said Winnie, interrupting her mother's daydream. "It has to be something suitable. I was thinking maybe –" she hesitated and looked hopeful – "that top hat Dad bought yesterday would be good?"

The colour drained from Lord Pepper's face as he clutched the edge of the kitchen table. "But I told you I only have nineteen top hats, which is hardly any," he protested in a high voice. "Couldn't we offer one of our mega-marrows? Or maybe a bramble cake?"

Lady Pepper patted his hand. "An antique topper would be a kind gesture, dear. With all those stars on it, it rather looks like it might have belonged to a performer, once upon a time. It really would be an ideal first prize."

Lord Pepper looked pained for a moment, then gave a reluctant nod. "I admit, the best prize would be a hat. Truthfully I can think of no better reward for…well, anything." He suddenly perked up and let out a snort of delight. "In fact, maybe I shall win it myself? Isadora, dear, look,

can you see my ears moving?"

"Splendid," said Winnie, handing over a small sheet of paper. "I'm glad that's settled. It will be happening one week from today, so is it all right if I start handing out these leaflets now?" Lord and Lady Pepper's eyeballs roved over the advert, like ants on raspberry jam.

"Golly, Winnie, these are smashing. We didn't know you were so artistic!"

"Oh, it's not me," explained Winnie. "It's the work of a very talented hare called Valentine. Do you remember? I've told you about him lots of times. He's very good at drawing."

Lord and Lady Pepper exchanged glances and smiled. Winnie often referred to her collection of invisible friends.

Valentine, however, looked delighted with the compliment. He nibbled the end of his paintbrush, batted his long dark lashes and said, "They do look splendid, don't they?"

Calling Bartonshire's Best!
Do YOU
Have a hidden talent?

Singers, dancers, jugglers, poets, magicians
(especially MAGICIANS)

Are Invited to perform at the

STARCROSS SHOWSTOPPER

Saturday 11th December at 10am
Starcross Hall, Bartonshire

Please send entries to Miss W Pepper at Starcross Hall
Interesting Refreshments Available

First Prize: An Antique Top Hat!!

Gabriel patted Valentine on the back with a wing tip. "Some of your best work, I'd say – especially your illustration of Wish's hat. There can't be many starry ones like that around. It's a long shot, but you never know. It might jog a certain someone's memory, eh?"

The Beloveds made four hundred flyers, filled up Winnie's bicycle basket and watched her cycle into the distance with the mission of pinning them all around Bartonshire.

That day and the next, Winnie posted them in the public library, through people's letter boxes and stuck them to lamp posts; anywhere that Ernest Salt might see them.

Soon entries began to flood in. Every day that week after school, Winnie and Knitbone dragged the mail sack upstairs, tipping an avalanche of entries out onto the attic floor. There, waiting to deal with the mountain of paperwork, was a production line of Beloveds.

First it was Martin's job to slice open the envelopes with his sword and whip the entries out. Then he handed them to Valentine, who in turn read them aloud whilst Wish typed out their details *clickety clack* on his typewriter. Finally Gabriel filed them all neatly in alphabetical order and then handed the entry forms over to Orlando, who polished his spoon collection with them.

"It says here that Mrs Tuppence would like to enter her gargling cat," said Valentine, "and Mr Wilson the vet says he can do a really good impression of a sticky toffee pudding."

"Goodness me. The standard is terribly high," honked Gabriel. "I had no idea we had such gifted individuals on our doorstep."

Winnie tapped her foot impatiently. "We've got lots of applications all right, but nowhere is

there one from a boy called Ernest." She looked
at the calendar and nibbled at her nails. "There's
only one day to go. He's had nearly a week to see
the leaflets in town – why hasn't he entered?"

Wish checked his
compass. "He
will come,
Winnie
Pepper.
I'm certain
of it. Be
patient."

Orlando
smiled and
wriggled closer to

the hat. "Orlando is patient. He know that one
day hot-cross bunny will love him and kiss him
and hug him." He fluttered his eyelashes at Wish.
"Slowly-slowly-catchy-bunny."

Wish looked appalled. "FOR THE LAST

TIME, PLEASE CONTROL YOUR MONKEY!"

"Hang on!" said Valentine holding up a piece of paper. "What's this?"

"Look!" cried Winnie, reading the entry form and waving it above her head in delight. "Abracadabra! E Carbuncle – Magican!"

Chapter 11

SNOW BUSINESS

On the day of the talent show, everyone was woken by a deafening chorus of bells. They'd stayed up past their bedtime getting the ballroom ready, hanging bunting, setting up a stage and laying the chairs out in neat rows, so Winnie set four alarm clocks to make sure they didn't oversleep this time.

Feeling rather shell-shocked, Winnie sat up in bed, looked around her room and immediately sensed that something was different. The wardrobe, the rug, the dressing table, the bookshelf, the posters on the wall – they were all the same but she was certain that something had changed. Eventually it dawned on her. The light in the room was odd. It wasn't gloomy and grey like it had been for days, but on the other hand, it wasn't quite like bright sunshine either.

Winnie slipped out of bed and crossed over to the frozen window. She rubbed her warm hand on the pane of glass. The ice melted, causing her to gasp in delight at the sight before her. "It's SNOWED!" she cried. "Quick, everyone, come and see!" Martin, Gabriel, Valentine, Orlando and Knitbone bounded off the bed and jumped onto the sill. It was true; overnight Starcross had become a winter wonderland. The whole world was white, from the house steps to the tops of the trees.

"Isn't it *beautiful*?" gasped Winnie.

"What a scene!" woofed Knitbone.

"What a vision!" honked Gabriel.

"What a pretty picture," sighed Valentine.

"What a disaster."

A voice came from behind them. Wish had popped up in his hat, as white as a snowball.

Orlando held up his hands in confusion. "Wot duz bunny mean? Snow iz fun. Snow iz funner than fun."

"Oh no!" said Winnie. "Of course! How could I be so silly? Today's the talent show!" Winnie's delight had turned to despair in an instant. "The lane will be blocked! We are miles from anywhere. How are all the contestants supposed to get to Starcross?"

They all gazed out at the endless sea of white. The snow fell steadily in big fat flakes, drifting past the window like blobs of cotton wool. "You can't even see the courtyard any more," groaned Winnie. "The snow looks like it's very deep and it's showing no sign of stopping."

Normally this was not so bad. Normally, a snow day meant they could go tobogganing down the steep slopes that surrounded the house, building igloos and snowmen, having snowball fights, not to mention their favourite winter activity of all – ice skating on the river.

But today things were different. Today was Saturday. Today they needed the sun to shine and the driveway to be clear and the buses to run like clockwork.

"Let's not give up hope just yet," said Winnie, as Wish covered his eyes in despair. She pulled on a warm jumper, a duffel coat, thick leggings, woolly socks and a pair of wellies. "Maybe the main road's clear and cars can somehow still get through," she said, tying her hat under her chin. "Come on, Knitbone, let's set out on an expedition to the end of the lane and see."

The two explorers ventured out into a blank world, like tiny pencil drawings on a sheet of paper. An ordinary onlooker would have seen only one set of footprints in the snow, not knowing that a faithful ghost dog was alongside, high stepping and licking the white flakes as they landed on his nose. Winnie struggled down the lane, marvelling at the meringue-like drifts banking up against the hedges, emptying her pockets of crumbs for the hungry birds as she went.

When Knitbone and Winnie eventually

reached the bus stop, she was shocked to see that only the top bit of the pole was sticking out of the snow. She cast her eyes towards Bartonshire but there were no cars, no bikes, no walkers. The world was eerily silent, as if they were the only two souls left in the world.

"Well, Knitbone, we might as well face it." Winnie sighed. "No one's coming to show us their talents at Starcross today. It's over. We'd better go home and break the bad news to poor old Wish."

They turned to leave, when Knitbone stopped
and cocked his head to one side. "Whassat?"
he woofed.

"What's what?" asked Winnie, kicking at
the snow.

"Listen," said Knitbone, straining his ears.
"I can hear...bells."

Winnie lifted the ear flap of her knitted hat
and listened as hard as she could. At first it was
no more than a whisper; a high, silvery ting-ting.
Then it became more of a steady jingle and

jangle. Winnie scampered up the snow-covered hedge and swung off the top of the bus-stop pole to get a better view. "Oh. OH!" she gasped. "Knitbone – you won't believe what I can see!"

There, in the distance, pulled along by a pair of whinnying shire horses, was a red and silver sleigh, carving through the snow. As it got closer, Winnie could see it was full of the people of Bartonshire, bundled up in hats and scarves.

There was Library Jane, the lady from the café
and teachers from her school. Behind it were
even more people on skis and toboggans,
scooting through the snow. As they all got closer,
Winnie and Knitbone could hear the sound of
voices singing:

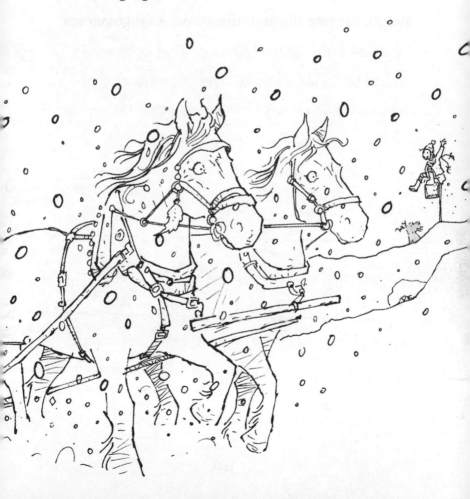

"WE'RE ALL GOING TO STAAARCROSS,
TO WIN THE TALENT SHOW,
WE'RE ALL GOING TO STAAARCROSS,
EVEN IN THE SNOW!"

"Look, everyone! Over there!" cried John the postman, jingling the reins. "Winnie Pepper is waiting for us at the bus stop! I told you we'd make it. Didn't I say so? The post always gets through!" There was a huge cheer and everyone waved. Despite the bitter cold, Winnie's heart filled with sunshine.

Chapter 12

CURTAiN CALL

The large crowd bustled through the doorway and spilled into the hallway of Starcross. Lord and Lady Pepper appeared and started taking everyone's steaming coats, seemingly not at all surprised that the contestants had turned up.

"Welcome, one and all," laughed Lord P. "The *snow* must go on, eh! Do have a toasted conker cracker."

"Oh yes," trilled Lady P, passing around a tray

of brown drinks, "and a warming glass of rhubarb and nettle juice too – spicy, sharp and hot. That'll set the taste buds tingling, all right! First time my dear husband tried one he couldn't feel his face for a fortnight, ha ha!"

Library Jane quietly poured hers into a plant pot. John the postman was not so lucky and ended up cramming fistfuls of snow in his mouth to cool down his tongue. On the whole, the atmosphere was very jolly.

"Registration's over here!" called Lady Pepper, pointing with her pen. "Come and get a number." She looked at the clipboard left on the table. "Oh, look at this, Hector, it's all been typed out. And do you know, I don't even remember doing it. How smashing."

Wish stood up in his hat on the landing and scanned the crowd, his nose twitching nervously. "Is Ernest here yet? Because I can't see him," he fretted, wringing his wispy paws. "He said he was coming! He sent in an entry form. Why isn't he here?"

"There's quite a crowd," said Martin, standing next to him. "Don't worry, I'm sure he's here somewhere. What does your compass say?"

Wish took it out and gave it a brisk shake. "Silly old thing is spinning like mad," he fretted. "I bet it's broken now too," he wailed. "Why must everything I own be an antique?"

Winnie and Knitbone appeared in the hallway and closed the big oak door behind them. She hung up her coat and scarf and the two of them followed the crowd into the ballroom, ready for the talent show to begin.

Wish's jaw dropped and his monocle fell out. "WHY HAVE THEY CLOSED THE DOOR? Not everyone is here yet!"

He hopped out of his hat and pressed his face between the banisters, as the assembled crowd took their seats in the ballroom. "STOP! We can't begin – Ernest hasn't turned up!" He took out his compass again and thumped it with his paw. "And just look at that," he wailed. "Now the stupid thing's jammed!"

Just as Wish was about to hurl his compass

down the stairs in a
temper, the front door
creaked slowly open again.
A hat bobble appeared
around the edge and a tall,
skinny boy slipped in
through the crack, as shy
as a whisper. He peeled
off his snowy coat and
long knitted scarf. Then
he straightened his bow
tie, patted his pockets
and checked his bag of
tricks. Finally, after what
seemed like an age, he
took off his woolly hat
to reveal a sight that Wish
had been waiting years
to see: a shiny thatch of
black curls.

Chapter 13

STAGE FRIGHT

Winnie stood on the stage, now in her party clothes. She gripped the microphone tightly in both hands, blinking into the bright lights. "Hello and good morning, everyone!"

The microphone let out a shriek and everyone covered their ears. Gabriel sat at the back and twiddled knobs on the sound desk until it stopped.

"Sorry about that, just a couple of technical problems. Showbiz, eh? Um, as you might know,

I'm Winnie Pepper." Lord and Lady Pepper
wolf-whistled and clapped loudly at the back.
"Thank you so much for coming out in the
snow to watch and take part in the Starcross

Showstopper! We have many amazing acts for you today, so without further ado I shall introduce you to our first entry." She looked down at the sheet of paper and said, "Please give it up for Mrs Tuppence and her amazing gargling cat!"

The gargling cat was indeed a triumph; the audience clapped and clapped. From then on the acts followed in a steady stream. Next up was Mr Topper's Miniature Flea Circus, which might have been very good if only anyone could have seen it. There was an ear-splittingly loud bit of opera by Seraphina Buckle, the lady from the pet shop. Whenever she hit a top C, glass shattered in various rooms around the house. At one point Lord Pepper had to dash off and drape a blanket over the best crystal.

Then it was the Beloveds' turn. There had been much debate between them over their act. Should it be scary or funny? Was it a problem that they were invisible to everyone but Winnie? As everyone had heard the rumours about the ghosts of Starcross Hall – they had been in the local newspapers after all – they decided to make a feature of it.

Winnie stepped onstage. "Ladies and gentlemen, girls and boys, I give you – the Spirits of Starcross!"

Knitbone leaped onto the piano stool and began to play a piece by Beethoven. He'd begun learning the piano to pass the time, way back when he was freshly ghosted. Over the months he'd become rather good. His paws still weren't quite the right shape to reach the notes and Martin had to jump up and down on the pedals for him. Nevertheless, he was very pleased to be able to show off his new skill. But to the audience it simply looked as if the piano was haunted. They gasped and applauded, marvelling at such clever trickery.

Then Orlando entered stage left, trailing a silk scarf, flouncing it around and throwing it into the air. He pranced and he danced, he twirled and he cartwheeled, scampering and pirouetting across the boards. "He's very excitable today, isn't he?" whispered Knitbone suspiciously. "I don't suppose anyone's been keeping an eye on the biscuit tin?"

His tummy stuffed with
naughty pink wafers, Orlando
took his freestyle dance
moves into the
audience, sharing
his talent

with all, causing much shouting and
screaming. Things got out of hand very
quickly.

"Orlando, come back! Stop it – NO! That's my
teacher!" said Winnie, grabbing the little monkey
as he scampered up Mr Best's trouser leg. Mr Best
squealed and leaped onto old Mrs Tuppence's lap,
squashing her cat and getting his bottom bitten in
the process.

Valentine tried to save the day. He grabbed the
microphone and began to sing "Twinkle Twinkle
Little Star" but this just seemed to make people

even more frightened. He had been going for perky, but instead the effect was whispery and downright creepy.

"Do you think I need more practice?" he said to Gabriel over the microphone, looking at the rows of horrified faces. "Maybe I should try a haunting rendition of 'Ring-a-ring-of-Roses'?" Some of the people in the audience began to weep.

"Oh, come on," bellowed Martin, who couldn't believe the audience were making such a fuss. "Cheer up, you ol' misery guts!" He took out a packet of biscuits and hurled them one by one into the crowd like missiles. "Have a ginger nut!" If there had been anyone left remaining

who wasn't screaming, they were now. People
were clambering over each other, heading for the
door in a panic.

Winnie looked anxiously around the room.
She was so used to ghosts these days she'd
forgotten that other people found them
frightening. Luckily Lady Pepper came to
the rescue.

"Goodness gracious, everyone in the audience, *please calm down!*" she cried, standing on her chair. "You are silly! You can't believe there are *real* ghosts here! This is the twenty-first century, you know! Do please return to your seats. It's just a clever trick! Very convincing. I say, *well done*, Winnie – here's to our very own Starcross illusionist! Hoorah and bravo!" She began to clap and soon everyone else joined in, enormously relieved and laughing that it was all make-believe after all.

"Phew," said Winnie, patting Knitbone's head. "That was a close one."

"Well, we brought the house down, all right," chuckled Gabriel, waddling down the aisle, Orlando gripped in a headlock under his wing. "Maybe we should do this more often."

Chapter 14

FOUNDLING

The talent show got back into full swing and act after act appeared onstage; singers, musicians, whistling piglets, mind readers and knife-throwers. Winnie cast her eye around the hall. This was all very enjoyable but they had a job to do. They needed to locate Ernest.

"He must be here somewhere. Martin said he'd arrived," said Knitbone, sniffing the air. "But where is he?"

Winnie thought for a moment and smiled.

"I bet I can guess," she said. "Follow me."

As they entered the Starcross library, they could see Ernest, gazing up at the portraits and the rows of old books. Winnie closed the door quietly behind them and cleared her throat. "Hello," she said shyly. "I'm Winnie Pepper."

The boy swivelled around in shock. "Oh, sorry!" he stuttered. "I probably shouldn't be in here, should I? It's just that I love a library." He looked up at the shelves in wonder. "You have so many books."

"I suppose we do, although it's rather old-fashioned in comparison with the brand-new public library in town," said Winnie, crossing the room towards him.

His eyes widened and he pointed at her. "Ah! That's where I recognize you from. You're the girl with all the astronomy books."

"Yes, yes I am," blushed Winnie, staring at the floor but secretly pleased that he had remembered. There was a long and awkward pause whilst they both tried to think of something to say.

Finally, Winnie broke the silence. "You're the boy that was looking for books on magic," she stuttered. There was another long and awkward silence. "Is that what you are planning to do today? Magic tricks? Is that your talent?"

The gangly boy took the wand out from his top pocket and scratched his head with it. "Well, I don't know that I have a talent for it really. This is my first competition actually." He smiled apologetically. "Sorry, how very rude of me.

I should introduce myself. My name is Ernie Carbuncle." He held out his hand and Winnie shook it.

"Do you mind if I call you Ernest?" said Winnie, pulling herself together. "It seems more…you."

"If you like," he said, looking a little perplexed. "But that's not actually my name."

Wish's top hat balanced on the mantelpiece clock. "I imagine you would like to win that hat," said Winnie, nodding in its direction. Ernest blinked at the top hat. He was sure it hadn't been there a minute ago.

Winnie smiled and sat down on the hearthrug. "There are lots of strange things about this house, Ernest. I could tell you some stories that you wouldn't believe."

"I've heard it's supposed to be haunted," he said, sitting down next to her.

"I've heard that too," smiled Winnie, looking

over at Knitbone. "People do say the strangest things, don't they?"

Ernest looked up at the hat again. "It's even nicer than I thought it would be. The silver embroidery is so shiny."

"So *are* you here to win it?" asked Winnie hopefully.

"Those are my orders."

"Orders?" said Winnie, suddenly confused. "That's a funny thing to say. What do you mean?"

"I have to win it for someone else."

The Beloveds were taken aback. This was unexpected.

"But…" said Winnie. "You're the talent. Who else would you be winning it for?"

"My parents," said Ernest, expertly spinning his wand around his fingers. "That's why we're in Bartonshire. They heard it was for sale in Finbar's Antiques Emporium and drove all night, but when we got there it had already been sold.

They were absolutely steaming, I can tell you. They even came here and tried to buy it, but a lady in an apron told them to go away."

"So *that's* who that was at the door last week!" said Winnie, remembering her mother's words about pushy strangers in moth-eaten furs wanting to buy her father's hat. "But I don't understand. Why do *they* want the hat?"

Ernest shrugged. "Dunno. All I know is that they've always been searching for one just like it; collapsible, old, stars on the side. They are obsessed by it. When they saw the competition leaflet they jumped up and down with excitement. I've never seen them so happy. It was wonderful – they stopped shouting at me for a whole five minutes. I was even allowed two bowls of bone broth for tea. It was one of my best days."

Knitbone growled and remembered the two people, pushing and shoving each other down the drive. He was smelling a rat.

"Like they say," said Ernest, "I'm *very* lucky really to have been adopted by parents that take such good care of me, considering how stupid I am. Apparently my real mother disliked me so much she tried to drown me at sea! The Carbuncles saved me from the waves and have taken care of me ever since then, even though it was very inconvenient and costly for them. 'No wonder she didn't want you,' they'd say, 'you silly gangling fool. Bad blood you've got and no mistake. Not surprising you haven't got any friends.'"

Ernest gave a small crooked smile as he straightened his knitted bow tie and looked down at his patched shoes. "Although to be fair, we move about so much it is quite difficult to make any."

"No," gasped Winnie.

Ernest looked at Winnie in astonishment.

"It's all true, I'm afraid. The Carbuncles have sacrificed everything to take care of me. They tell me all the time, so it must be true. The least I can do is win them the hat. In fact, they are here today to make sure I don't mess it up."

Knitbone growled. "Something doesn't feel right."

Orlando scowled and shook his fist. "Monkey show them a thing or five."

"Well, Ernest, you seem like a perfectly nice and clever person to me," stated Winnie.

"Really?" he said, standing up straight. "Nice? Clever? Do you *really* think so?"

"Yes," said Winnie, blushing furiously. "You

have a friendly smile and cheerful hair. Your bow tie is very unusual and individual. You also like books and libraries. I am very surprised that you don't have lots and lots of friends." Suddenly she blurted out, "I should be proud to be your friend. In fact," Winnie swallowed hard, "perhaps one day you would like to come here for tea?"

"Me? Here? With you?" he said with a splutter and a giggle that came out as a snort. "Well, I think that's just about the most smashing thing I've ever heard, thank you very much." A grin spread right across his face like a sunbeam.

Knitbone stared hard at Winnie and then he scowled at the boy. What was going on? He thought they had agreed that Winnie was not going to invite *anyone* for tea. Anyway, everyone knew that it was his job to sit next to her at teatime. And not only that, "smashing" was one of Lord Pepper's words and Knitbone didn't take kindly to it being used willy-nilly.

"WINNIE!" he barked, a little louder than was absolutely necessary. He pointed his nose at the clock on the mantelpiece. "PLEASE FOCUS."

"Hmm?" said Winnie, looking at the time and realizing it was getting late. "Oh, oh, yes, right. Let's get on with it. Focus. What are these 'parents' of yours called by the way?"

"Their names are Enid and Royston Carbuncle," answered Ernest. "They are out there, sitting in the audience right now. In fact they'll be wondering where I've got to. They don't like it when I wander off." He turned towards the door. "I really must go."

"But wait, Ernest…" protested Winnie.

"Actually," smiled Ernest, "this talent show opportunity is *such* a coincidence, because, guess what? My parents used to be magicians too! I found some old photographs tucked away in the bottom of one of the suitcases. Their stage name was The Tricky Two."

"Is he SERIOUS? THE TRICKY TWO? I remember them." A horrified gasp flew out of the hat. "Those halfwits with the rubbish stage name and no talent?" said

Wish, springing to his feet. "So *they* were the couple on the beach that day?" His eyes widened as the truth began to dawn. "Oh, *now* I see! So that's what they're up to!" Wish slapped his forehead. "What a fool I am. All this time I thought I was hunting Ernest, when in fact that rotten, cheating duo have been hunting ME!"

Chapter 15

THE IMPORTANCE OF BEING ERNEST

Ernest made for the door and Winnie knew the truth couldn't be put off any longer. She took a deep breath and said, "Ernest, don't go yet. I need you to listen carefully because I have something very important to tell you."

The boy looked anxious. "I really must go. They'll be looking for me. Enid and Royston will be raging if I miss the chance to win the hat."

Winnie plucked the wand from his top pocket

and held it up it. "Do you ever wonder where this came from?"

"It's just an old one of Royston's," said Ernest, looking down at the wand in Winnie's hand. "He said it came out of a Christmas cracker. I liked it, so they said that if I was good it could be my present for five birthdays and six Christmasses."

Winnie looked steadily into Ernest's eyes. "What if I were to tell you that the initials on the side are actually yours?"

"No," he said, shaking his head and looking a little crestfallen. "Oh dear, I see you have forgotten my name already. My name is Ernie Carbuncle, remember? EC not ES."

Winnie smiled. "Your name is not Ernie Carbuncle. Your name is Ernest Salt."

Ernest looked at Winnie quizzically. "No, it's not. I just told you."

"Listen carefully. Your *real* name is Ernest Salt, of the magical family Salt."

"Oh, now I SEE what's going on here, Winnie," said Ernest with a rueful smile. "Oh dear. You've mistaken me for somebody else, I'm afraid. The Salt family were a famous dynasty of magicians but now there aren't any left. In fact I was reading about them in my library book. Now, let me see if I can remember." Ernest screwed his eyes with the effort. "It was a tragedy I think. A family – a lady and her baby boy –

were lost at sea. They always used a particular top hat… Oh… OH!"

Ernest opened his eyes and found himself staring directly at the top hat on the mantelpiece. "OH!" He hurriedly opened his magic bag and took out a library book called *Magicians of the World* and flicked through the pages until he came to the relevant page. The caption read:

The celebrated magician Marigold with her baby son, Ernest, the last of the Salts. Both tragically lost in an accident at sea.

There was a photo of a smiling woman holding a laughing baby. The woman was very tall and thin, with a mop of black curly hair. The baby, who had exactly the same hair as his mother, clutched an ebony and pearl wand in his fist.

Winnie handed Ernest a magnifying glass from the shelf. "Have a closer look." Ernest took the magnifying glass and inspected the picture. The hat was covered in embroidered shiny stars and just visible on the side of the baby's wand were two engraved letters. Two letters that now quite clearly did *not* stand for *Easy Shop*.

Winnie looked sympathetically at the boy, gazing at the page. "I'm so sorry, Ernest. It's true that your poor mother was swept away. But the Salt baby – you – were saved from the waves."

The boy looked up from the page. "By the Carbuncles?"

"No, not by the Carbuncles, that's just what they told you. Your life was saved by Wish Salt." She paused, knowing that the time had come. She reached up onto the mantelpiece and took down the hat. "Ernest, hold this."

Ernest reached out his hands and obediently took the hat.

"Now, we must be quick. In order to officially reunite the two of you, I need you to make three wishes."

"Reunite who? Who is Wish Salt?" asked Ernest. "Winnie, you're talking in riddles."

"Please, Ernest," said Winnie, an eye on the door, the distant cheering loud as yet another act ended. "Please just trust me. Please," she begged. "We're friends, aren't we? This is very important."

Perplexed, Ernest scratched his head with the wand. "This is turning out to be a very strange day. But it's true that you are my friend, the first and only one I have ever had. I do trust you." Ernest took a deep breath and began. "Firstly I wish I could live in one place. Secondly I wish this hat was mine, and thirdly, I wish I knew who this Wish Salt was."

The hat suddenly collapsed flat in Ernest's hands. It popped up, then down, then up again. It hummed, buzzed and spluttered, as a rainbow of miniature fireworks went off inside. Red, green, pink and gold sparkles bloomed out of the hat like flowers, cracking and whizzing until there was nothing left but a veil of curling smoke and eventual silence. Ernest coughed and waved at the air.

When the smoke cleared, in it stood a small figure, one ear up, one ear down. He bowed smartly and adjusted his bow tie.

"Wish Salt, at your service."

Ernest stared at the small figure and laughed in delight. "*You* are Wish Salt? But you're a... *rabbit!*"

Wish straightened his monocle and shook out his ears. "Technically I am a talking ghost rabbit." He gave a stiff little bow. "I am also a professional magician and guardian to the family Salt."

But Ernest wasn't listening. He reached out a hand to touch his snowy-white fur. "What a sweet-looking little bunny," he crooned. "Look at your twitchy pink nose and soft silky ears!"

"Oh, *er*, no," said Winnie in alarm, "I wouldn't do that if I were you. Wish doesn't like to be touched. He's an Heirloom Beloved, you see, a spirit animal that devotes itself to the protection of a whole family, not one person. He's more like a bodyguard than a pet. A personal assistant. A security officer, if you will."

Ernest, paying no heed to Winnie's warning,

reached into the hat and lifted Wish into his arms. He stroked Wish's ears and kissed his little nose and told him how special he was.

The Beloveds braced themselves for the protests, for the denials, the refusals and the complaints. But instead, something very strange happened; Wish went floppy. He closed his eyes, his whiskers drooped and a big, wistful smile crossed his face.

"What's happening?" asked Wish, his voice dreamy. "Am I ill? Do I have a temperature? I feel sparkly in my nose and sunny in my toes. I know there is work to do but...this really is extraordinarily pleasant."

"Well, well. Would you believe it?" chuckled Valentine. "It looks like the reuniting has turned you into a normal Beloved, just like us. We clearly have more in common than we thought. My dear boy, it looks like you have finally found your special person."

"No, no, that's not possible. There must be some mistake," murmured Wish, his eyes glazed with bliss. "But what is this peculiar sensation?" he said, as Ernest stroked his ears. "This feeling of happiness and safety? This feeling of home?"

"Oh, you silly-billy funny-bunny," squealed Orlando, hurling himself at Wish and hugging him so tightly his rabbit eyes bulged. "EEZ LOVE!"

Chapter 16

BACKSTAGE CREW

Winnie decided it was time to quickly introduce her new human friend to her ghostly animal ones.

"This is Orlando – he's a monkey – and this is Martin the hamster. Over there is Gabriel the goose and Valentine the hare. And right next to me is my very own Beloved, Knitbone Pepper. He's a dog."

Knitbone sat in a sulky silence.

"I'm sorry, Winnie, but I can't see them,"

whispered Ernest, his eyes wandering around the room, trying to fix on something. "Am I doing it wrong?"

"Oh no, that's perfectly normal," smiled Winnie. "No one can see them except for me. I can see all of the Beloveds everywhere, all the time. That's *my* talent, I suppose. But they can see you as clear as day. Please feel free to say hello." So Ernest did, most politely.

"Charming boy," crooned Valentine.

"Salt of the earth," agreed Martin.

"Such a winning smile," said Gabriel.

"Salt and Pepper go together!" giggled Orlando. "What you think, woof-chops?"

"He's all right, I suppose," said Knitbone with a sniff. "If you like that sort of thing." Mrs Jones's words still rang loud in his ears and he gulped down a whine in his chest.

With an eye on the clock, Wish told Ernest everything. He told him all about his great-great-grandfather, Joseph Salt, about the magic shows, about the dying wish and the family secret. He told him all about the theatres and the halls, the brightly lit stage performances and the glowing newspaper reviews. Then he finally told him the true story of the sinking of *The White Rabbit* and his quest to find him.

"So…my real mother *wasn't* horrible after all? And she *didn't* really think I was useless?" asked Ernest, a lump in his throat.

Wish put a soft paw on the boy's face. "Dearest Ernest, your mother was the very best sort of person. I can assure you she loved you very much."

"But why would the Carbuncles say such terrible things about her?" asked Ernest. Wish scowled and clenched his paws into fists.

"The Tricky Two were our rival magicians," he growled. "Never liked us. They were always hanging around, asking us what our secret was, always wanting to buy my hat, spreading silly rumours, following us from city to city like annoying flies. But finding a baby they KNEW to be Ernest Salt and not telling anyone? That really is wicked. Why would they do that?" Wish shook his head in regret. "And what are the chances that they should be waiting on that very beach, on exactly the same day as the shipwreck!"

"Unless..." said Valentine darkly, looking at Gabriel, "it wasn't a coincidence at all."

"What can you mean?" asked Wish. A look of horror crossed his face. "Oh no! Surely not. You can't be suggesting that..."

"CALLING CARBUNCLE!" Lord Pepper barged into the library. "Is there an ERNIE CARBUNCLE in here?" He looked at the two children standing by the hearth. "Ah, Winnie. Is your friend a Carbuncle? There's a very unpleasant couple out here in a proper rage searching for him!" He looked down at his clipboard for a moment. "It says on my list that you're a magician? Is that right? Come along. The audience is waiting and you are the last act. Quick as you can!"

The boy magician took a deep breath. Ernest Salt picked up his magic bag and marched into the ballroom, ready to take to the stage.

Chapter 17

IF THE HAT FITS

Outside the light was fading fast. Throughout the day the snow had continued to fall and the audience were checking their watches, keen to be home safely before dark. There was just one more act to go.

Ernest took a black silk cape out of his bag, slung it over his shoulders and stepped straight into the glare of the spotlight. "Ladies and gentlemen, welcome to my very first magic show." He cleared his throat nervously. "Today you will witness sights that will astound and amaze you." Winnie clapped and whooped, causing everyone to turn and look.

"First, a little sleight-of-hand magic." Ernest held up a gold coin, then rolled it along his knuckles back and forth, back and forth. Suddenly it vanished, only to appear in the palm of his other hand, bright and shiny. There was a polite round of applause. Next, he pulled a bunch of brightly coloured paper flowers out of his sleeve. More polite applause.

"I need two members of the audience to come

up onstage to help me with my next trick," said Ernest, turning left and right, casting his eye around the crowd. "What about you two over there? Yes, you! The couple in the rabbit-fur coats." Gabriel swung the spotlight onto a pair sitting on plastic chairs right at the back. Knitbone's hackles shot up in alarm as he recognized them straight away. They were definitely the strangers that he had seen bickering in the driveway days before.

The woman knitted her eyebrows together in disapproval and pursed her lips.

"No, thank you," said the man, shielding his eyes from the bright lights. "I don't think so."

As soon as he spoke the hat collapsed, as flat as a pancake, in Winnie's hands. She tried to prise it open but it was locked firmly shut. Knitbone had a sudden thought. Was the hat trying to hide itself from the Carbuncles?

"Oh, come on," said Ernest, "don't be shy.

Everyone, please give them an encouraging round of applause!"

Lord and Lady Pepper lifted the reluctant couple to their feet and propelled them to the stage as everyone clapped.

"So," said Ernest, looking rather nervous, "what are your names?"

"You know our names, you clot," hissed the woman, grimacing at the audience through lipstick-stained teeth. "We are Enid and Royston Carbuncle, of course," she simpered. "Your dearly beloved parents."

Ernest turned back to the audience. "Ladies and gentlemen, I give you Enid and Royston Carbuncle!" Everyone applauded politely. "Thank you for taking part in this revealing magic trick," said Ernest. "For it I shall need a hat. Does anyone have one I could borrow?"

"Yes, I have!" said Winnie on cue.

She skimmed the flattened top hat over the audience's heads. "Will this do?" she shouted.

It sliced through the air and Ernest caught it like a frisbee. In his hands it popped straight back up. "Why, yes," he said. "This very hat will do the job nicely!"

As they caught sight of it, the Carbuncles gripped each other's hands tightly. The famous Salt magic top hat! This was the moment they had been waiting years for and the excitement made them sweat like a pair of old cheeses.

Ernest turned to his volunteers. "Enid and Royston, do you have any thoughts about what may be inside this hat?"

"It better not be a rabbit, that's for sure!" roared Royston. They cackled and wheezed with laughter.

"I know, a saucepan! No, a pot plant!" said Enid excitedly, her thick white make-up splintering across her grinning cheeks.

"No, no," whispered Royston. "We must think of something better. We've waited a long time for this moment. Challenge the boy with something bigger. A ladder or…or a garden rake… or a bicycle!"

"Well, let's see what's inside, shall we?" Ernest bowed to the audience and as he stood up he spoke quietly into the hat, "Wish, *it's showtime.*"

Ernest reached his arm down into the hat, right up to his elbow.

"ABRACADABRA!" he cried, as he hauled out a long wooden ladder, pulling it up rung by rung. The Carbuncles tittered with excitement and clapped their hands in delight. Soon a bucket, a set of candlesticks, a rolled-up carpet, a garden rake and a hula hoop followed. The audience went wild! The boy had talent!

"Thank you, thank you, you are very kind. Now, does anyone here have a pocket watch I may borrow for my next trick?"

"We do, Winnie," honked Gabriel. "Remember the gift from Bertie Tombellini?" Winnie reached into her pocket and felt the familiar cool disc in her palm. She took it out and passed it to the young magician.

"Ah," said Ernest, taking the watch and reading the inscription on the back. "*Friendship is Timeless.* Perfect." He turned to the audience. "Ladies and gentlemen, hypnosis is an ancient art. Today I will hypnotize these two members of the audience…in fact, you may be surprised to learn that I have already begun. Sleight of hand, you see." With a sweep of his arm he gestured behind him. "Behold: the Carbuncles."

Indeed, the two sat stock-still on their chairs. They stared straight ahead, like giant stuffed rabbits on display. Enid gawped and Royston's mouth hung slackly open, a strand of drool trailing off the end of his moustache.

Everyone marvelled at Ernest's hypnotic skills. "His showmanship is very good, don't you think?" whispered Gabriel. "I mean, for a beginner."

"Ah," said Valentine sagely. "But it's in his blood, isn't it? Don't forget – he's no Carbuncle. We're witnessing the magic of the last true Salt."

Ernest dangled the pocket watch in front of the Carbuncles, their gaze swinging back and forth, back and forth.

"Enid and Royston Carbuncle," he said. "Let us go into the dark mists of your past, back, back, many moons ago. Now, tell me, do you remember a family called…Salt?"

The Carbuncles frowned, their faces contorting. It was as if their minds and their faces were locked in battle, as they desperately tried to keep their dark secret in. But the effect of Ernest's hypnosis was too strong, their eyes as wobbly as grapes in jelly. Enid clutched her handbag, her red mouth pinched up, the truth dribbling out of the corners.

"Disgusting. Typical Salts. I heard a rabbit *died* in that hat," she shuddered. "Nasty little rodents. No good for nothing but coats and cooking pots. We offered a very fair price for it, considering. A scrub with bleach and it would be as good as new. But, oh no, those Salty stinkers wouldn't sell their precious magic hat for any amount. 'That hat is part of our family,' Marigold said. 'It won't ever leave us and we would never part with it. Anyway, there would be no point because the hat will always find us. Now for the last time go away.'" Enid snorted in disgust and one of her fake eyelashes fell onto the floor like a spider.

"Anyway, I ask you, how can a HAT be part of a family?" barked Royston. "Specially one that whiffs of dead bunnies."

"That was when I knew," said Enid. "It was as

plain as the nose on his face. We wanted that hat, and she wouldn't give it to us, so really what happened served 'em right." She leaned towards Royston and whispered very slowly and loudly, "We shall have to be very clever though, dear. Such a tragedy. Nobody must suspect. Then the stupid Salts will be gone for ever and the hat will be ours."

Royston idly poked around in his ear with a dirty fingernail. "All it took was a few little holes carefully drilled in the bottom of that boat and then they were sunk."

"We stayed up all night on the beach, happy as clams, watching and waiting for the hat to wash up on the tide with the seaweed, dreaming of our future," murmured Enid. "And suddenly, there it was, on the shoreline!" Her eyes suddenly narrowed. "But the snivelling SALT BABY was in it."

"How it survived I don't know, waving its

little stick," growled Royston. "'Run!' said Enid. 'Forget the kid. Grab the hat, you idiot!' But we were too late. A wave stole our hat, and we were left with a brat. It had all gone wrong."

"But then I remembered Marigold's words," hissed Enid, her face brightening. "'Our hat will always find us!'"

"Oh, you're such a rotter, Enid," tittered Royston. "Of course! The kid is just the wormy bait we need to lure our magic hat back. And he won't even know that he's a Salt, will he? It's not as if there's anyone left to tell him. He'll just think he's one of us, a little maggot on our Carbuncle hook." He crooked his finger menacingly at the hat. "Come here, little fishy…"

"Hat and Salt, Salt and hat. All ours for the taking. But shhh, dear one…" She held her knobbly finger to her thin lips, her eyes flicking from side to side. "We must never tell anyone.

It must be our secret. Finally we will be the greatest magical family in England."

They clutched at each other and laughed, gurgling and spluttering like blocked drains.

There was a shocked silence in the audience as everyone looked at each other in confusion. Was this part of the show? Or was it some sort of awful joke?

"BOOO!" shouted
Valentine.

"What villains!"
honked Gabriel.

"MAKE THEM
CLUCK LIKE
CHICKENS!" shouted
Martin, shaking his sword.

Orlando said nothing.
Instead he climbed up onstage and slowly
cartwheeled into Enid's handbag. Within
seconds, Enid and Royston's eyes began to
redden and stream as Orlando delivered his
own brand of rough justice; a carefully crafted
stonking stink, arising from deep within the old
used tissues and half-sucked sweets. As the
sickly green mist seeped out and slid up the
Carbuncles' hairy nostrils, with all the muscular
determination of an eel, Orlando somersaulted
merrily offstage.

As he did, Ernest wheeled a large black box out of the darkness of the stage wings. It was covered in stars and had the word SALT painted on the side in swirly letters.

"Hang on a minute, where did that come from?" whispered Winnie.

Knitbone wagged his tail. "Looks like the work of a certain magic rabbit to me."

"And now, ladies and gentlemen, for my final trick," said Ernest, turning to the audience, a slight tremor in his voice, "I intend to make these wicked criminals disappear FOR EVER!"

But Ernest had not noticed that the heel of Enid's stiletto had begun to twitch.

"Oh no-no-no, Ernest!" cried Winnie. "They're waking up!" Unfortunately Orlando's stonking stink was so powerful it had had the effect of shaking the Carbuncles from their trance.

"Oi! What's going on here?" snapped Enid, coming to her senses, questions shooting out of her like a machine gun. "What's happening? What have I been saying? What's that stench? What's that watch? What's that box? If you think I'm getting in there then you're stupider than you look. Seeing as you look very stupid indeed, that is saying something! Shut up and give me that hat so we can get out of this dump."

"No."

"No? NO?" Enid's eyes popped and she went bright red with rage. "Don't you DARE say no to me, Ernie Carbuncle. Did you hear that, Royston? After all we've done for you. After all we've sacrificed out of the goodness of our hearts." She snatched at the hat. "Give me that!"

"NEVER," bellowed Ernest. "I know the truth! How could you be so wicked? That's the last time the Tricky Two tell me what to do."

Royston made a grab for Ernest's cape. "Come 'ere, you little weasel," he roared. "Oof!" Suddenly Royston felt a violent explosion in his midriff. Then in his arm. Then his head, his leg, his elbow, his nose. "Ow! Argh! What's that? Ow!"

Wish had flown out of the hat in a fearsome rage and had begun to launch a series of ninja flying kicks on Royston.

"Ow-ow-ow-ow!" screamed Royston. "What evil is this?"

"Ah. This must be the *natural warrior* bit the book talked about," said Gabriel, folding his wings knowingly.

"You fool!" screamed Enid. "Stop messing about. We haven't got time for this."

The audience stood up in their seats and began to boo loudly. Some of them had screwed up their paper programmes and began to pelt the Carbuncles with them. Others threw their leftover conker crackers.

Martin grabbed a pink wafer from the sideboard and took a big bite. "Don't worry, Ernest and Wish – you're never alone with a ghost! Remember: a Beloved in need is a friend indeed! S.O.S. stands with you. *CHARGE!*" The hamster dashed up the steps and sank his sharp teeth deep into Enid's ankle.

"AAARRGGHH!" she wailed. "Pierced by the sharp fang of wickedness! Save me, Royston! I told you, didn't I? I always said that boy was rotten to the core." Enid reached out and grabbed Ernest by the ear. Now limping, she began to drag him offstage, hissing, "Just you wait until I get you back to the van. I'll tell you something for nothing, boy, you'll be sorry you *didn't* drown on that day when I've finished with you."

Winnie looked frightened for her friend. Knitbone growled; a low, dangerous rumble. He wasn't exactly Ernest's biggest fan, but Enid Carbuncle had gone too far. Nobody upset Winnie and got away with it.

Knitbone leaped up on the stage, barking and snarling for all he was worth. He grabbed the microphone cable in his teeth, dragged it across the stage and wrapped it around and around

Enid's ankle. He gave the cable a yank and, with a strangled squawk, she fell backwards on top of her husband. As they toppled into the open box like a pair of dominoes, Wish whistled through the air and slammed the lid shut with a flying kick. Then, with lightning reactions, Ernest slid the three bolts across the door and smacked the box hard with his wand.

"*ALAKAZAM!*"

A shocked silence fell on the stage like
a curtain.

Ernest took a deep breath and turned to
the audience. He picked up the hat and placed it
carefully on his head, finding to his surprise that
it fitted perfectly. Then, stepping to the front
of the stage, he began.

"There's been a wicked crime
Which wasn't my fault.
I was *never* a Carbuncle.
I am the true
ERNEST SALT!"

The box bolts suddenly flew back and the
lid burst open to reveal a ticker-tape rainbow
blizzard. But there was no sign of the
Carbuncles. They had simply vanished into thin
air, leaving nothing but a few stray rabbit hairs
on the floor and the smell of singed fur.

The crowd burst into a rapturous round of applause and Lord Pepper strode up onto the stage and shook Ernest's hand.

"Well, that really WAS amazing! Never seen anything like it! I suppose we really *should* find out where those revolting people have gone, but unfortunately we have run out of time! I believe we have a clear winner of the Starcross Showstopper. I, for one, cannot think of anyone who suits that hat more. Ladies and gentlemen, I give you the magician and winner of the competition: ERNEST SALT!"

The audience clapped and cheered, none more loudly than Winnie and the Beloveds. Ernest and Wish took a sweeping bow together – the first of many to come.

"Now, quickly, quickly," cried Lord Pepper, handing out coats and scarves. "Look at the time! The snow is falling and soon it will be dark. Everyone to the sleigh and toboggans!"

Chapter 18

BEST FRIENDS FOREVER

As everyone clambered onto the sleigh, did up their ski bindings and strapped themselves onto their toboggans, Lady Pepper handed out hot baked potatoes to be tucked in pockets. These served the dual purpose of keeping everyone warm and providing a tasty snack should they get hungry on the way home. It had been such a wonderful day and everyone agreed that Lord and Lady Pepper should put on a talent show every winter. People marvelled at

how toasty and welcoming the old house was, even though the weather was so cold.

As the crowds drifted away, Winnie and Ernest stood on the steps smiling at each other. "Thanks for coming, Ernest," said Winnie shyly. "I've had a really nice time."

"Nice? I have had the very best day of my life," said Ernest, his curls poking out from under the top hat. "To think that I believed I was worthless and useless." He turned to look down at Wish, who was snuggled in his coat. "Now I know that I mattered to Wish all the time. I can't tell you what a difference that makes to a person, just to know somebody cares. And now, as if that wasn't enough, I have a terrifically special human friend too. Winnie, thank you so much for, well, everything." He giggled and tucked his wand in his top pocket. "Maybe it's fate with names like ours. We do go together, don't we? Salt and Pepper, Pepper and Salt!"

Winnie laughed. "We certainly do, like two shakers on a tablecloth! Maybe it's written in the stars. But what will you do now, Ernest, now that the Carbuncles are gone for ever? Where will you live? You're just a child after all and *somebody* has to take care of you." Her expression suddenly changed. "You're not going away, are you?"

"Oh, don't worry. Library Jane has said I can live with her," said Ernest. An apple-cheeked lady in a red coat sat in the sledge, smiling and beckoning for him to sit next to her. "Did you know she lives right next door to the library?" he said. "In the pretty blue-gabled house? She says she'll enrol me in the school now I've got a real address. Maybe we could even sit next to each other, Winnie? In fact, Jane says you're welcome to come to tea any time, seeing as we both like books so much. You could come over after school every day." Ernest immediately went bright red. "But that's only if you'd like to, of course," he stuttered. "I mean, you don't have to."

"Well…I would really like to come to tea," said Winnie shyly. "We could have our own book club and talk about stories over crumpets. At the moment I'm reading a really good one about interplanetary travel but…"

"Oh yes," nodded Ernest. "That does sound good. I can't wait to hear about that. I'm reading about cutting people in half and I'd really welcome your ideas."

Knitbone watched this brand-new friendship blossom before his eyes and sorrow welled up inside him. He knew he should be pleased for Winnie but he just felt sad, his tail drooping and his head hanging low. It was taking all his willpower to hold in a desperate, heartbroken howl. Mrs Jones had been right all along; one day Winnie wouldn't need him any more. He just hadn't expected it would come so soon.

Noticing their friend's sad face, Orlando cuddled his leg and Martin offered him an emergency ginger biscuit.

"Actually, hang on a minute," added Ernest thoughtfully, stroking Wish's ears. "I can carry Wish anywhere in the hat, but I've just remembered that Knitbone can't leave Starcross, can he? Those are the Beloved rules, aren't they? They are tied to their home? How thoughtless of me, Winnie. You wouldn't be happy without your best friend, would you? Anyway, Knitbone was the hero who saved the day with his quick thinking back there, toppling the Tricky Two into the box. Maybe we could meet at your house after school instead?"

Knitbone's ears sprang up and his tail began to wag. *What was that? What did he just say? That Knitbone was a hero? That he was still Winnie's best friend? That they were going to meet at Starcross?*

Winnie laughed with relief. "That would be much, much better. I love spending time with Knitbone. He's the kind of dog that makes everything better, just you wait and see!"

Knitbone shot into the air like a furry rocket. The howl burst out of him, but now it was one of pure joy. Knitbone danced and pranced around the hallway, Orlando  and Martin clinging onto his fur like they were on a bucking bronco. "SHE LOVES ME SHE LOVES ME SHE LOVES ME SHE LOOOOOVES MEEEEEEEE!"

Curses spilled out of the vase in the hallway.

"Did you hear that, Mrs Jones?" said Knitbone, woofing as loud as he could into the vase. "In your miserable fangy-face! But of course, I never believed a word you said. I will always be Winnie's best friend forever. SO THERE!"

Chapter 19

A FEAST OF FRIENDS

As the clock on the mantelpiece struck four, Lady Pepper wheeled a trolley into the Starcross library. It was laden with all manner of strange and delicious snacks: sea-sponge fingers, scones with violet cream and wild strawberry jam, quail's egg sandwiches, honey jelly, apple crisps and fizzy pumpkin pop.

"Teatime!" she trilled, parking the trolley next to the roaring fire. "I've included a large plate of biscuits too, three different sorts as requested."

Then Lord Pepper appeared around the doorframe, carrying a wobbly tower of hat boxes. "Thought I'd bring some hats for you and Ernest to try on, not to mention a selection for all of your invisible friends to choose from, eh? Can't have too many chums."

"Thanks, Mum and Dad." Winnie smiled as her parents retreated to the ballroom. "You're the best. See you later!"

The table in front of her was covered in a crisp white cloth and set with eight places. At the far end of the table sat Ernest, eyes boggling at the splendour that lay before him; antique silver platters, cutlery, candlesticks, soup bowls, tea plates, dinner plates and crystal jugs and goblets. "This is amazing, Winnie," gasped Ernest. "It's so posh!"

"Is it?" asked Winnie, unloading the trolley onto the tablecloth. "It's all very old. This is just what's in the cupboards."

Lining the edges of the table, perched on a range of booster cushions, were the Beloveds. Martin already had a tiny napkin tied around his neck, knife and fork in his paws, licking his lips.

"Right, Spirits of Starcross," said Winnie, tossing a ginger biscuit into Knitbone's mouth. "Don't be shy, tuck in!"

With a high-pitched battle cry, Martin launched himself at the feast, cramming biscuits

sideways into his cheeks. Gabriel scoffed three chocolate biscuits and promptly fell asleep. Valentine thought it was very funny to pour a jug of pumpkin pop over his head to wake him up. This all ended in a massive mushroom muffin fight. Then Orlando dragged his handbag around the table and stole everyone's spoons. Wish had a pink wafer biscuit and ended up bouncing in the jelly. Even the hat was happier. Everyone noticed

that now it didn't have to hide from the
Carbuncles, it hardly ever broke down any more.

Eventually tea was over. Ernest patted his
tummy and cast his eye around at the mayhem.
"Yum. Those honeycomb buns were the most
delicious thing I've ever tasted in my whole life," he
said. "Is teatime at Starcross always this exciting?"

"Well," giggled Winnie, taking a hat out of the
box and placing it on her head, "here at Starcross

we never do things by halves. Do you want to play a zombie board game? We've got lots of pieces but none of them quite match so we'll have to make up our own rules."

"Nothing new there, eh?" said Valentine with a wink.

The rest of the afternoon passed happily as Winnie and Ernest played Snakes-'n'-Scrabbleopoly in front of the fire. Gabriel quizzed Wish on his filing systems, and was even allowed to have a go on his typewriter. Martin built an impossibly tall tower of biscuits and Orlando snoozed on the hearthrug, carefully licking custard from his fingers. Meanwhile Valentine sat in the corner of the room, sketching.

"What are you drawing?" asked Knitbone, peering over the hare's shoulder.

"I'm sketching all of us together," said Valentine. "Do you like it?"

Knitbone looked hard at the picture. They all

looked so happy in it, as if things had always been this way. But Knitbone knew different. He still remembered a lonely, sad time; before he was invited to join the Beloveds, before he and Winnie were reunited. He had been certain then he would be alone in the wardrobe forever. Yet here he was, with more friends than he could ever have dreamed of. He looked over at Winnie and Ernest sat together, laughing and joking and he wagged his tail like a windscreen washer. Knitbone felt all warm inside, but this time it was nothing to do with the fixed boiler.

Seized by happiness, Knitbone jumped up onto the table and barked, "I want to make a toast."

Suddenly awake, Orlando sprang up beside him and tapped a crystal glass with a silver teaspoon. "LISTEN, COZ WOOF-FACE IS A-SPEAKIN'." He turned to Knitbone and bowed most politely. Gabriel, Valentine, Martin,

Orlando, Wish and Winnie all waited patiently
for their friend to speak.

Knitbone cleared his throat. "I just wanted say
how lucky I feel to be with friends, old –" he
looked over at Ernest and wagged his tail –"and
new." Ernest couldn't see him do this of course,
but Winnie's face lit up like a lantern, and really
that was all that mattered.

"Please raise your ginger nuts," barked
Knitbone. He balanced his biscuit carefully on
the tip of his nose, only to suddenly toss it into
the air and scoff it in one big snap.
"To adventure, to fun and TO THE
MAGIC OF FRIENDSHIP!"

Collect ALL the adventures of

KNITBONE PEPPER

GHOST DOG

Meet **Knitbone Pepper,** the lovable ghost dog!

KNITBONE PEPPER
GHOST DOG

Best Friends Forever

Knitbone has made lots of new animal friends since becoming a ghost dog. But his owner, Winnie, is missing him.

Can the ghostly gang come up with a plan in time to help Winnie see Knitbone again?

Roll up! Roll up!
The circus is coming to Starcross!

KNITB🐾NE PEPPER
GHOST DOG

The Last Circus Tiger

Winnie and her ghostly animal friends can't wait. The magicians, acrobats and clowns are such fun!

But Knitbone sniffs something beastly in the big top...

Meet Moon,
Knitbone's new friend!

KNITBONE
PEPPER
GHOST DOG

A Horse
Called Moon

One starry night, Winnie and Knitbone Pepper
find a ghost horse hiding in the garden. Her name is
Moon, and she is searching for her long-lost owner.

But Moon has a spooky secret,
which is sure to spell trouble.

Look Who's Landed!
A human ghost!

KNITB🐾NE PEPPER

GHOST DOG

The Silver Phantom

Winnie and Knitbone Pepper are thrilled when a vintage plane lands at Starcross Hall, bringing with it Martin the hamster's beloved ghostly owner.

But this visitor is a human ghost - and that means mischief!

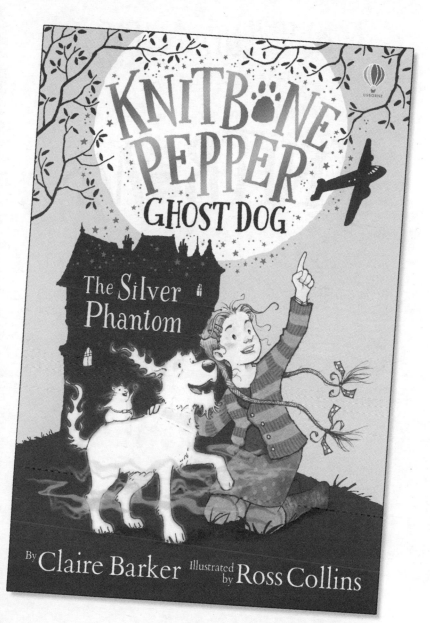

By Claire Barker   Illustrated by Ross Collins

MEET THE AUTHOR

Claire Barker is an author, even though she has terrible handwriting. When she's not busy doing this, she spends her days wrestling sheep, battling through nettle patches and catching rogue chickens. She used to live on narrowboats but now lives with her delightful family and an assortment of animals on a small, unruly farm in deepest, darkest Devon.

MEET THE ILLUSTRATOR

Ross Collins is the illustrator of over a hundred books, and the author of a dozen more. Some of his books have won shiny prizes which he keeps in a box in Swaziland. The National Theatre's adaptation of his book "The Elephantom" was rather good, with puppets and music and stuff. Ross lives in Glasgow with a strange woman and a stupid dog.

First published in the UK in 2019 by Usborne Publishing Ltd.,
Usborne House, 83-85 Saffron Hill, London EC1N 8RT, England.
usborne.com

A CIP catalogue record for this book is available from the British Library.

ISBN 9781474953535 JFMAMJJ SOND/19 05124/1
Printed in the UK.